TERRIFYING SHARK TALES

Written by Scott Ingram

Illustrated by Ron Rundo

ROXBURY PARK

LOWELL HOUSE JUVENILE

LOS ANGELES

NTC/Contemporary Publishing Group

Published by Lowell House
A division of NTC/Contemporary Publishing Group, Inc.
4255 West Touhy Avenue, Lincolnwood (Chicago), Illinois 60712-1975
U.S.A.

Lowell House books can be purchased at special discounts when ordered in bulk for premiums and special sales. Contact Department CS at the following address:

NTC/Contemporary Publishing Group
4255 West Touhy Avenue
Lincolnwood, IL 60712-1975
1-800-323-4900

ISBN: 0-7373-9855-8

Roxbury Park is a division of NTC/Contemporary Publishing Group, Inc.

Managing Director and Publisher: Jack Artenstein
Editor in Chief, Roxbury Park Books: Michael Artenstein
Director of Publishing Services: Rena Copperman

Printed and bound in the United States of America
00 01 02 DHD 10 9 8 7 6 5 4 3 2

Table of Contents

For Miles and Abby

—S.I.

Beyond the Reef

Park Ranger Heather Burke picked up the handset. "The Great Barrier Reef stretches more than 1,250 miles along Australia's northern coast," she announced over the intercom as the glass-bottom boat hummed slowly over the spectacular underwater seascape. A few dozen passengers crowded into the glass chamber hanging six feet beneath the square, slow-moving platform. Heather noticed some people in the group wearing T-shirts with the names of colleges in the United States. "For our American visitors," she added, "the reef covers an area equal to about half the size of Texas."

Hank Longley looked with wide-eyed amazement. "It's not just one long plain of coral, is it?" he asked.

The ranger smiled back at Mr. Longley, a stocky, pale man who, after just a few hours in the Australian sun, had acquired a sunburned nose that glowed above his black walrus mustache.

"No, sir," she said. "It's more like a connected group of smaller reefs. There are about 2,500 in all."

Taller and darker than her husband, with salt-and-pepper hair that hung to her shoulders, June Longley raised her eyebrows in wonder. "From the air, it looks like it goes on forever," she said.

The Longleys were on vacation with their children Luke, 15, and Cara, 14. They had arrived that morning at a resort in Cairns, a town in North Queensland, Australia. Ahead of them lay two weeks of sun, swimming, and snorkeling in the "eighth wonder of the world." The Longleys had planned—and saved for—the trip for several years. In fact, ever since they'd seen a documentary about the Great Barrier Reef, they'd started what they called a "reef travel fund," putting away every extra penny from birthdays, baby-sitting, tax returns, and bonuses so they could take their dream vacation.

They had snorkeled at home in Connecticut to prepare for diving in the clear turquoise waters that covered the reef. But after the first few minutes of gazing out of the glass across the rainbow spectrum of countless varieties of fish, they knew that diving in the murky waters of Long Island Sound could never have prepared them for the jaw-dropping beauty of what lay before them. Cara Longley pressed her nose against the glass as the boat passed over a stretch of coral that looked like a green, leafy salad.

"Lettuce coral is the name given to the formation we are now passing over," Ranger Burke said, as if reading Cara's mind. "And off to the left is fire coral, which, as its name suggests, can give unsuspecting snorkelers some painful cuts. It's razor sharp."

Luke Longley yawned. This tour was okay, but it wasn't very exciting. Sure, you got to see the reef up close and personal. And yeah, it was like being in a reverse aquarium. But he wanted to see something else.

Where are the sharks? he wondered. *I like coral and angelfish and stuff. But I could see them at Marine World back home. I want to see sharks—big, monstrous man-eaters!*

Luke raised his arms above his head to stretch. He was still tired from the long jet ride halfway around the globe from his home in New England. He had just decided to leave the crowded viewing area to go take a nap when he turned and bumped into someone right behind him. Startled, he found himself face to face with a girl about his age with the most beautiful, copper-colored hair and green eyes he'd ever seen.

"G'day," the girl said with a blinding smile and an accent that said she lived here in the Land Down Under.

"Uh . . . sorry," Luke said shyly. "I didn't know anyone was behind me."

"No problem. I didn't mean to crowd you. I just wanted to get a better look at the coral. I can't believe this reef is made up of billions of skeletons."

"Huh?" Luke grunted. "What do you mean, *skeletons*?"

"That's what coral is," the girl explained. "Limestone skeletons of living creatures. Incredible, eh?"

Luke nodded in amazement. Not amazement over the coral—he knew what it was—but over the girl. He'd never seen anyone quite so beautiful.

Don't stand there like a dummy, he scolded himself. *Ask her what her name is!*

"I'm Rachel," she said, as if reading his mind. She held out her hand. "Rachel Crossdale."

Luke breathed a sigh of relief and took Rachel's soft palm in his. "Luke," he mumbled. "Luke Longley."

"Luke! Did you see the—" Cara had pushed through the crowd to talk to her brother. But she stopped when she saw that he was . . . uh, busy.

Rachel smiled. "Hello. You must be Luke's sister. You look just like him." She extended her hand. "I'm Rachel Crossdale."

Cara smiled back. She wasn't used to kids her age acting so grown-up and formal. She awkwardly shook Rachel's hand. "I'm Cara. Luke's sister." She giggled. "Oh, right. You figured that out already."

Luke caught his sister's eye and gave a slight sideways jerk of his head that said *Get outta here*. But before Cara could take the hint, their mother and father pushed next to them, trying to get closer to the window. Rachel introduced herself, then tugged at the sleeves of a tall, sunburned man and a slim, red-haired woman. Luke could tell right away they were Rachel's parents.

As the Longleys and Crossdales exchanged greetings, Luke noticed that Mr. Crossdale shook hands left-handed, keeping his right in his pocket. The adults seemed to hit it off right away, and while they chatted it came out that both families were staying at the Wellington Arms. Luke smiled at Rachel. This was going to be an awesome vacation.

"We're coming to the outer edge of this section of the reef," Ranger Burke's voice came in, breaking through the chatter. "Beyond this point, the Coral Sea drops off hundreds of feet."

Everyone pushed to the window and looked into the dark

blue of the deep ocean—everyone except Luke. He couldn't take his eyes off Rachel. Standing behind the crowd pressing against the glass, he watched her auburn hair sway back and forth as she spoke to Cara and pointed at sea creatures that caught her gorgeous, green eyes.

"As the reef slopes down, you'll notice a number of creatures," the ranger went on. "There are some spiny sea urchins off to the right, and if you're careful you might spot a moray eel or two. They nest in the area and have a nasty bite. But don't worry. They're really quite timid—unless disturbed."

Luke daydreamed about how he might impress Rachel as his parents and the Crossdales chatted about hometowns and businesses, and Rachel and Cara chattered away. It worried him how Cara was monopolizing her time. He'd met Rachel first, and now he felt like the odd man out.

Ranger Burke's voice came over the intercom once again. "We'll be heading back momentarily. But before we do, let me call your attention to the large mollusks off to the left. They are giant clams. Some are three feet across and weigh up to a thousand pounds. Notice what happens as the boat's shadow passes over them."

Ooohs and aaahs rose from the crowd. Luke ignored the group and gazed out at the open sea. *Who cares about clams?* he thought bitterly. *I want to see sharks!*

"Look at that!" Rachel exclaimed. "The clams snapped shut. Our shadow made them close."

"Yeah, cool," Cara said. "Maybe we could wave some cocktail sauce to get them to open up again."

Rachel chuckled, but Luke just sighed and stared into the

dark blue waters. *Girls!* he thought. Then suddenly he squinted into the distance at a dark torpedo shape.

"Hey, look!" he blurted. "Is that a shark out there?"

An anxious buzz rose from the group as all faces looked into the dark waters. Moments later, a gray shark about five feet long with black-tipped fins swam to the window, then banked left and glided along the length of the boat. Its cold eyes and slightly open mouth gave it the look of a demented killer.

Rachel turned away from the window with a look of wide-eyed terror on her face, and Luke edged closer to her. *She sure had a strong reaction to such a small shark,* he thought. *After all, there's no way it can hurt us in here.*

"The shark that just passed the starboard window was a reef shark," the ranger announced, keeping her voice even and calm. "They sometimes come to the reef to feed on the octopus that live here. That's their main food." She paused as she noticed some looks of concern among the group. "No need to worry for those who plan to snorkel. We are on regular shark patrol. No one is allowed in the water if there's any activity. And all rangers carry shark batons to ward off any unforeseen problems."

As the intercom clicked off, the shark made another pass at the window, its ghostly pale belly skimming along inches from the glass. Rachel drew back as though she had just received an electrical shock.

"Don't like sharks, huh, Rachel?" Luke asked from over her shoulder.

Rachel shook her copper hair as she looked down at the deck. "Can't stand 'em," she said shakily. "It's why we've waited so long to come to the reef for a holiday. I-I have nightmares."

"It's only a small shark," Luke said, trying to sound like an expert and comfort her at the same time.

Rachel looked at Luke and shook her head. He got the uncomfortable feeling that he had somehow put his foot in his mouth. Then she turned to her father a few feet away and tapped him on the shoulder.

"Daddy, Luke just told me that shark we just saw is *only* a small shark," she said sarcastically. "How big was the shark that—" She stopped and looked away from her father, tears welling in her eyes. She was unable to finish her sentence.

Mr. Crossdale turned to face Luke. He held his hands four or five feet apart as though measuring the length of the shark Rachel was referring to. As he spread his arms, Luke's eyes focused on the man's right hand—or what was left of it. Mr. Crossdale had only a thumb and index finger. In the area where his other fingers and palm should have been, there was just empty space. Mr. Crossdale's hand was like a pincer with a plum-colored band of flesh attaching it to his wrist.

"It happened when Rachel was five or six," Mr. Crossdale explained without waiting for Luke to ask. "We were at a beach outside of Sydney."

Just then the boat jerked as its engines reversed and it turned back toward the inlet where it docked. Mr. Crossdale paused and looked out of the glass into the dark ocean as if remembering the incident. Luke saw several more torpedo shapes in the distance but didn't say anything. Instead, he listened carefully to Mr. Crossdale's story.

"I saw some bloke in a wet suit swimming far out past the surf line—maybe a hundred meters," Mr. Crossdale continued.

"Suddenly he began struggling. It looked like he was having trouble keeping his head above water."

As Rachel's father went on with his story, other people in the cramped glass room turned from their underwater sightseeing to listen. Luke saw that Rachel and Mrs. Crossdale had their arms around each other's waists as though the memory was too frightening to recall alone.

"I was closer to the man than the lifeguards were. And I'm a strong swimmer." Mr. Crossdale smiled proudly. "In fact, I used to be a lifeguard in my younger days."

Luke wasn't surprised that Mr. Crossdale had been a lifeguard. The man had the lean, broad-shouldered build of a well-conditioned swimmer. Although Luke was the top freestylist on the Madison High swim team as a freshman, he had the distinct feeling that Mr. Crossdale could swim circles around him—mutilated hand or not.

"Anyway," Mr. Crossdale went on, "I grabbed a board and paddled out as quickly as I could. When I got close I saw why the guy was struggling." Mr. Crossdale paused and ran his left hand through his thinning sandy hair. "He was surrounded by sharks—'only small ones,' as you put it, Luke. They were reef sharks drawn in close to shore by who knows what. Regardless, they had the poor fellow in a real predicament. He grabbed for me, and I saw that the right arm of his wet suit was empty and shredded. I reached into the water to get hold of him, and suddenly a shark rose straight up between us."

Rachel let out a half-choked sob and sat down. Mrs. Crossdale looked at her husband with concern. "Do you really think we should tell this story now, John?" she asked.

The hushed attention of the people in the glass room answered her question. Mr. Crossdale *had* to finish the story.

Speaking softly as if remembering the pain, he went on. "Before I could react, I felt a pressure on my hand—a weight yanking it down deeper. My arm was into the water shoulder deep. Then another shark hit me . . . here." Mr. Crossdale pushed up the sleeve of his shirt. At his elbow was a deep, purplish hole. It looked as though the muscles had been torn away from the joint, leaving only the bone and a thin layer of scar tissue.

"There was blood squirting everywhere—like a fountain. Naturally, I went into shock. I looked at my hand and wondered, Is that my hand?" Mr. Crossdale laughed and looked at the crowd as if he'd made a joke. "Luckily, the lifeguards were close by in a longboat. They got me and the other fellow back to the beach. He was in bad shape—worse than me. When they unzipped his wet suit his body was in pieces, and he bled to death within half an hour. I was lucky. They flew me to a hospital and patched me up." Mr. Crossdale nodded to his wife and daughter. "My wife and daughter saw everything. They saw what *small* sharks can do."

Cara looked at her parents and shuddered. Luke felt his face burn. The horrible story didn't frighten him as much as it made him feel ignorant. He'd made a fool of himself in front of Rachel— in front of everyone in the boat.

Boy, he thought, *my dream vacation is sure getting off to a lousy start!*

A week later, the Crossdales and the Longleys boarded a twin-

13

hulled catamaran piloted by Park Ranger Burke. The petite yet tough-looking young woman whom everyone called Heather piloted the two families about ten miles offshore to a long stretch of reef, not far from the area the group had seen their first day in Australia.

Luke tightened the diving mask around his head, clamped his teeth around his snorkel's mouthpiece, and slipped into the water lapping against the diving platform of the catamaran. Sighing with pleasure as the sea surrounded him, he floated on his back. They'd gone snorkeling a lot already, and he still couldn't get used to the bathwater warmth of the tropical ocean.

"How's the water, Luke?" Rachel called as Luke's head bobbed above the clear water. "Too cold, I hope. If it is, I've a good excuse *not* to go in."

Luke tried to smile, but the mask pressing down on his face held his cheeks in place. He pushed the mask up on his forehead and stood in the neck-deep water. "Sorry, Rachel, the water's perfect. It's even warmer than the pool back at the hotel."

"But there aren't any sharks in the pool, remember?" Rachel said, offering him a pouting face.

"There aren't any sharks out here, either," Luke countered. He pointed to the ranger, who was anchoring the boat and getting ready to come into the water. "Heather said no sharks have been sighted since that first day on the boat a week ago."

Then Luke pointed to his parents and to Cara adjusting their masks and snorkels. "Do you think my family would go snorkeling if they thought there were any sharks? Even *your* parents have been in every day."

But Rachel just shook her head. "Sorry," she called. "It's just not for me."

Luke noticed how seeing the shark that first day had put a damper on all of Rachel's activities since. While he, Cara, and his parents had spent every day exploring the wonders of the reefs with experienced divers like the park ranger, Rachel had shopped or sat by the pool reading. Even Mr. and Mrs. Crossdale had become frustrated by Rachel's reluctance to go into the water. Every day they coaxed her to go with them, then just ended up leaving her at the Wellington and going off with the Longleys. Today was the first day she said she *might* consider giving snorkeling a try. Everyone was just glad that she had decided to come out on the boat.

"Come on, Rachel," Luke pleaded. "I'll keep a special watch for sharks, and I'll let you know if I see even a hint of one."

Finally, after a little more coaxing, Rachel agreed to give it a try. Sliding gingerly into the water, she carefully let herself go under and in two swift strokes was next to Luke. Laughing, she spit out her snorkel and gave him a swift kiss on the cheek.

"You're right," she said. "The water *is* perfect!" She took Luke's hand and pulled him toward deeper water. "Come on! Let's not wait for the others."

"Hey, wait for me!" Cara cried as she saw Luke and Rachel swimming off. "I don't want to be stuck with the adults!"

"Hold on, you two!" Park Ranger Burke shouted through cupped hands. "The rules are you have to wait for—" She stopped and shook her head.

Luke and Rachel had already sunk beneath the surface, their Day-Glo green snorkels poking above the water as they paddled away.

Luke had a hard time keeping up with Rachel. She was a strong swimmer, like her father, and since this was her first day exploring, she was supercharged, gliding through the water as if she had gills. Luke looked back and saw that the rest of the group were so far behind they looked like tiny Day-Glo fish. He wanted to wait—but he wanted to be with Rachel more. Taking a deep breath, he headed out after her.

The water deepened to about fifteen feet as the two teenagers continued toward the outer edge of the reef. Luke followed Rachel as she dove to get a closer look at the darting flashes of silver and gold that were parrot fish, damselfish, surgeonfish, and all kinds of tropical denizens. Colors moved and shapes changed like a kaleidoscope before Luke's unbelieving eyes. There were abalone and anemones, sea cucumbers and urchins. And boy, was there coral—coral of every color in the spectrum!

Luke and Rachel swam farther and farther ahead, unable to contain their joy at the underwater wonders they were seeing, unaware of how long they had been in the water or how far ahead of the others they were. Luke felt his heart hammering in his chest, but he wasn't sure if it was from swimming fast or being alone with Rachel. She pointed to a field of coral off to their right and dove down toward it. Luke followed, his attention captured by the pinkish-orange coral floor.

In two swift strokes, Rachel had almost reached the coral bed. Luke was amazed at how strong she was, and wanted to show that he could move faster underwater than she could. When he was nearly beside her, he kicked his flippers and pulled hard with his arms, trying to reach the coral before she did.

But Luke misjudged both the distance to the coral and his own strength. Before he could stop his descent, he plowed into a protruding edge of the hard, pink, spiny limestone. For all of its delicate beauty, the coral had ridges as sharp as jagged razors. Luke groaned as he felt it tear into the thick meat of his shoulder muscle beside his collarbone.

Rachel turned when she heard Luke grunt through his snorkel. When she saw him suddenly rising to the surface in a cloud of air bubbles, she quickly rose up beside him. As her head popped above the water, she saw Luke wincing in pain.

"Luke! Are you all right?" she cried in a shaky voice. "I saw you hit that ridge of coral. You didn't break anything, did you?"

"Naw. But I sliced up my shoulder a little. Ow!" Luke exclaimed, as he treaded water and rubbed the bloody torn area on his shoulder. "Man, it really burns!"

"It was fire coral. Remember what Heather said the first day?"

Luke shook his head. "No. I wasn't listening." Luke smiled. "I was looking at you."

Rachel smiled shyly, but it faded quickly when Luke pulled his hand away from his shoulder and blood dribbled from his sliced flesh into the water. "You're *bleeding*!" she said, fear creeping into her voice.

"I'm okay. Come on, let's keep going." Luke was doing his best to ignore the stinging cut and the saltwater biting into it. He wanted to appear brave to Rachel, but it wasn't easy. His cut really hurt.

"Are you *nuts*?" Rachel asked in disbelief. "Don't you know you're not supposed to swim in the ocean if you're bleeding?"

Luke felt his face redden. He'd been so caught up in being alone with Rachel—and with acting tough—that he'd forgotten about sharks. Blood was a magnet for them. They could sense a drop hundreds of yards away. He looked down and saw a red cloud coloring the turquoise water around his shoulder.

"You're right," Luke said, trying to control a sudden wave of fear rising in him. "We'd better head back." He put his snorkel in his mouth—then stopped.

They looked at each other as the same thought struck them. They'd swum so far so fast, diving every which way, that they'd lost sight of the catamaran. Neither Luke nor Rachel was sure where they were. They looked for the snorkels of the others poking up above the water, but saw nothing but lapping waves. There were several shapes on the flat, turquoise horizon, but neither Rachel nor Luke could tell which speck was their boat.

Rachel's eyes widened under her mask and Luke knew that if she let fear beat her, they'd both be in trouble. He willed himself to remain calm.

"We have to swim away from the darker water," he said, gesturing in the direction of dark blue water. "We know that's where the reef ends."

Rachel nodded and smiled uncertainly. "They're probably looking for us right now," she said. "I'll bet my mom and dad are upset."

Luke nodded. "My folks are probably ticked off, too. Let's get going."

The two worried snorkelers began to swim back toward a speck that they thought might be the catamaran, making certain that the dark blue of deeper water was always on the same side—their left. Luke's shoulder pounded with pain as he plowed through the warm water, unable to keep up with Rachel, who remained a few lengths ahead. Nervously, Luke looked back every few minutes to make sure that sharks were not tracking the bloody trail he was leaving behind.

Suddenly Luke felt a tap on his right side. Startled, he glanced over and was relieved to see Rachel, who had slowed and was smiling as she pointed off to her right. Far in the distance were the tiny silhouettes of what looked to be several adults. She squeezed Luke's hand softly, and for a moment he forgot the dull ache in his shoulder.

But his relief didn't last long. Seconds later, Rachel's grip tightened and Luke heard a muffled scream coming through her snorkel. She let go of his hand and pointed frantically—no longer to her right, but to her left. Those shapes in the water that they had thought were human—they were torpedo shapes!

In horror, Luke saw a dark, wiggling mass of sharks moving from the deep water toward the reef, growing larger right before his eyes. *That's odd,* Luke said to himself, his numbed brain still managing to think. *The sharks can't be following my trail because they're coming at us from the side, not coming from behind.*

Fighting a new wave of panic, Luke squeezed Rachel's hand. Then he motioned for her to go on in the direction they thought the boat was in. As soon as the sharks caught the scent of his blood, they'd surely go after him, and maybe Rachel would make it to the boat.

But Rachel's fear was so powerful she began to shake her head back and forth hysterically, clutching Luke's good shoulder as though she were drowning. Determined to remain strong, Luke popped his head above the surface, grabbed Rachel by both shoulders, and forced her head above the water. Then he spit the snorkel from his mouth and shouted, "Get a grip, Rachel! You're a strong swimmer. Lead the way back. I'll follow at a distance. If the sharks get too close, I'll swim in a different direction while you bring help!"

Rachel shook her head, then spit out her mouthpiece and shouted, "No! No! I can't make it! The sharks will—" But her voice cut off as it rose into a shriek.

Luke shook her hard, paddling with his flippers to keep his head above water. "Listen to me, Rachel! You don't have a choice!" He grabbed the mouthpiece of her snorkel and pushed it gently back into her mouth. Then he shoved her as hard as he could away from the oncoming school of sharks and in what he hoped was the direction of the boat.

Back underwater, Luke fell behind Rachel as she cut through the water with powerful thrusts of her flippers. He tried to keep up, but his throbbing shoulder and the long swim had weakened him. By now he could see that the sharks were about the size of the reef shark he had seen on the first day. They were coming nearer and nearer, but they didn't seem to be in any kind of attack mode. In fact, it looked like the sharks were fleeing from something attacking *them*.

For a moment Luke pondered this. The only thing they would be swimming from was . . . something *bigger*!

At the very same instant that this terrible realization hit him, Luke saw the silhouette looming behind the school of sharks. It looked at least two or three times bigger than the prey it swam after. In fact, it looked like a giant bomber among tiny planes. Through the clear water and the shrinking distance, Luke saw dark stripes on the flank of the huge creature. Then, as it cut its way through the school of smaller sharks, he saw the blunt snout and sharp, pointed tail.

Tiger shark! Luke's mind screamed. He'd read about the ferocious man-eaters before the trip. They lived in shallow tropical waters and sometimes grew to be twelve feet in length or more . . . and they ate anything in their path. Luke's heart pounded as he recalled the picture he'd seen of the stomach contents taken from a dead tiger shark. Laid out on a dock were a coil of copper wire, a wallet, a dog's paw, and several wine bottles!

Luke had begun his vacation wishing to see a large shark, but now that he knew his wish was coming true he'd have given anything to see those boring tropical fish he'd scoffed at before. Hardly able to breathe, his fear rising in his throat, Luke watched as Rachel extended the distance between them. As far as he knew, she had not seen the tiger shark. He hoped she wouldn't. He hoped that she—

Suddenly Luke saw billowing clouds of blood. The tiger shark was slashing through the smaller sharks, ripping them to pieces. As the large shark dismembered the smaller ones, its prey also went mad with the smell of blood in the water . . . and a killing frenzy began.

As Luke watched in horror, hoping that he wouldn't become part of their meal, he saw that Rachel was far enough ahead to escape the slaughter. *His* fate, however, was not so certain. It was only a matter of time before the tangle of frantic and dying sharks would engulf him. He gulped a lungful of air and dove to the bottom. In swimming class he'd held his breath for over three minutes once. Now he'd probably have to hold it longer—his life depended on it.

If I can just stay perfectly still below them and remain unnoticed, he thought, *they're busy enough killing themselves to pass right over me.*

Crouching on the bottom, holding a ridge of coral to keep his buoyant body from rising, Luke watched in disbelief as a dozen small sharks shot over him like speeding missiles. Then his eyes widened in awe as the huge tiger shark swam by only six or seven feet over his head, the intestines of smaller sharks trailing from its jaws.

As the ominous shadow passed across his body, Luke knew this was his chance. But as he tried to rise from the coral bed, he felt a heavy weight holding him back. He couldn't move. Panicked, Luke looked down at his foot. A huge clam, its instincts triggered by the shadow of the giant shark, had closed tightly around his left ankle.

Frantic, Luke tried to slip his foot out of his flipper, but the thousand-pound mollusk had a firm grip. *This is it!* Luke's mind shrieked. *I'm going to die!*

As he fought against the pull of the clam, Luke felt his lungs about to burst. Then, suddenly he saw the tiger shark turn and whirl its monstrous body down toward him. In his oxygen-starved brain, he slowly realized that his frantic movements had caught the beast's attention. Nothing more than a helpless spectator to his own death, Luke watched as the green striped body zeroed in. Then, just before the creature slammed into him, he closed his eyes.

Instantly, the sound of cracking bone and tearing flesh echoed in Luke's head as he screamed. Then bloody bubbles rose to the surface . . . and Luke was rising with them.

Through the red plume trailing behind him like a rocket's exhaust, Luke saw sharks below surround the giant clam. They were all fighting for the morsel that dangled from its giant shell— it was a leg. Luke wondered whose it was. Then he saw blood jetting into the empty space below his knee. The last thing he saw before blackness swallowed him was a strange hand reaching out to him—a hand with just a thumb and an index finger.

"Luke! Luke!"

Through the haze of pain, Luke heard Cara's voice. Then he heard the sound of a helicopter. When he opened his eyes, his father and Mr. Crossdale were holding a tourniquet around the remains of his left leg. A paramedic readied an injection for the pain he knew he should be feeling, but Luke felt nothing except Rachel's tears splashing onto his face as she cradled his head.

"I couldn't—I couldn't move," he said, gritting his teeth. "I was trapped."

Rachel looked back beyond the reef. "Killers! Nothing but bloody killers!" she screamed.

"Killers." Luke whispered the word and closed his eyes as the injection did its work. Someday he'd have to tell Rachel how a killer had saved his life . . . from a giant clam.

A String of Kills

There is a splashing and slapping movement on the surface. The great creature senses the motion from hundreds of feet away. It turns, bending nearly in half, and propels its massive body from the ocean depths to the surface. On the top of its snout, its nerve cells, tiny openings filled with jellylike fluid, continue to sense the vibrations through the water and direct it toward the motion.

The beast has not eaten for many days. Now it is time.

The rough-skinned denizen of the deep swims rapidly toward its prey, thrusting its massive tail from side to side as it slices through the cold waters of the North Pacific. The chill has no effect on it. The fierce ruler of the oceans is able to raise its body temperature above that of the flesh-numbing waters. And the rise in body temperature only increases the speed and power of the beast's muscles. In seconds it is already warmed up.

Closer now to the motion on the surface, the giant's nerve cells, in its head and along its sides, detect a heartbeat. Receptors on the beast's snout sense the nearness of meat and warm blood . . . growing nearer. Now the monster's shiny eyes are reflecting light from the surface. Its acute vision zeroes in on the contrasting dark and light colors of the prey above. The current "meal" casts a long oval silhouette, with four thinner shapes extending outward—two on either side. All of these shapes move in unison, unaware of the killer that approaches from below.

Now on its final approach, the ascending beast reveals itself. First, a two-foot dorsal fin rises out of the water. Then, as the moment of attack nears, the creature turns, then dives straight down so that it can launch itself upward with an unstoppable, bone-shattering force.

Finally, the streamlined torpedo of terror rockets toward its target from below. The once-calm blue water becomes white and frothy as the giant bursts from the deep, its immense jaws open. A split second before the moment of impact, the beast's upper jaw dislocates from its head and it extends two rows of triangular, fist-sized teeth beyond its snout. A thin sheath of skin slides over the eyes like protective goggles. Everything is orchestrated for a perfect strike.

The creature is built to attack. And now it has hit a hundred-pound fur seal with the full force of its half-ton body. Twisting and ripping through the seal like a butcher's cleaver through butter, the killer shark ignores the seal's bark of surprised horror. For the beast is feeding, slicing its razor-sharp teeth through layers of fur and fat, rupturing arteries and snapping its meal's spinal cord like

a twig. Cut in half, the floundering seal gushes blood into the water as its attacker retreats a short distance to consume its first morsel and to wait for the victim to bleed to death.

In moments, the seal's blood has spread out across the ocean. The upper half of its pudgy body shudders helplessly as exposed nerve endings twitch and die . . . and then the second strike comes.

Taking the remaining chunk of the seal's body into its gullet, the monster is finally satisfied until it must feed again in a few days. Only a red stain dissolving on the blue water and scattered chunks of fur offer a clue that any other creature once swam there.

Now the killer returns to the chilly depths to continue its endless journey. It must move constantly, forcing water through its gills to pull the oxygen from the water, the oxygen that it needs for its massive body to survive. The pursuit and attack of its meal has taken only minutes.

There is a splashing and slapping movement. The giant creature ignores the fish swimming nearby. It is more interested in the movement on the surface, movement that is accompanied by a flash of light and color. The emptiness in the creature's belly has returned, and its guidance systems lock onto its colorful prey. It is time to feed . . . again.

Teeth lost in the last killing have been replaced. Now a new crop of razor-sharp triangles has sprung up from the endless rows of teeth lying beneath the skin of the jaw. Yes, the beast, built for attack, is ready.

As before, the prey's silhouette is oval, with four thinner shapes extending outward—two on either side. This time, however, the creature's meal will be larger.

Guided by its nerve cells, the killer moves toward the surface, drawn by the prey's vibrations. Closer now, it senses a heartbeat and begins the final run at its target, powering its massive body faster and faster through the wave-tossed ocean. It shows the warning fin, submerges, turns, then explodes upward, a thousand pounds of fury backed by a crushing set of jaws.

There is a horrifying scream. Unlike the seal's bark, it is louder, shriller, full of panic. There is no fur, either. It is a different kind of prey, and the beast's systems give it this information. Now the cutting edges of its teeth must saw through rubber, flesh . . . and Styrofoam.

Retreating with particles of flesh clinging to its teeth, the creature senses blood billowing in the water and detects exposed meat. Meanwhile, the prey is thrashing. It must be dragged under the waves in order to squelch its frantic movement. The beast rises for the second strike . . . and to complete its meal.

There is a splashing and slapping movement—only now it is the creature itself that makes it. The giant is struggling, but cannot free itself. A thin web has wrapped around its huge body. The more it struggles, the tighter the filaments bind themselves around its tonnage. Soon the creature is trapped in a cocoon that will keep it from moving, from pulling the oxygen it so desperately needs from the water. The powerful beast has met the only opponent that can defeat it . . . and soon the beast will drown.

The creature's gills open and close in an exhausted attempt to breathe. Water *must* flow past the huge slits on either side of its body. The beast cannot survive if it is motionless, and now that it is, its nerve cells are dying and its guidance systems are shutting down. The last sound the dying creature hears is a mechanical hum on the surface. There is a tugging, and the creature dies as it rises out of the water with the help of a gigantic crane.

"Hey, Fred! Look! Look what the net dragged in!" A grizzled deckhand points excitedly to a trailer-sized net bulging with thousands upon thousands of shiny, wriggling fish . . . and something else. The net is suspended from a steel boom at the stern of a fishing trawler. The huge ship has steamed across the chilly waters of the North Pacific for months, dragging in and processing tons of fish daily.

"Drop the net here on the deck, Charlie," Fred says, tossing his cigarette overboard as Charlie operates the levers that turn the boom and lower the net. "That looks like . . ." His mouth drops open. "It can't be!"

"It is," Charlie says excitedly, as he and Fred yank the huge tail of the creature, sliding it out from beneath the silvery, wriggling mass. "It's a great white."

Charlie and Fred look at each other, then crane their necks upward to look at the wheelhouse high above the deck. No one has seen what came with today's catch. Quickly, the two men move to separate the shark from the other fish and free it from the net. Then they drag the giant beast out of view.

Fred grunts as he pounds the shark over and over with a thick wooden club to make certain it is dead. Charlie, in the meantime, is taking care of the rest of the catch. He raises the boom, closing the net back around the wriggling mass of fish, then swings the huge steel arm over the opening that leads below deck. His job done, Charlie slips into the shadows, where Fred has already begun preparing their surprise catch for slaughter.

"Man, we can make us some extra cash on this," Fred says, straddling the shark and stabbing a thick gaffing hook through its snout to pull it back. "Look at those jaws! Get the knife, Charlie. The big one."

Charlie grabs the handle of a huge, jagged, blood-stained blade, and with both hands he jams it deep into the shark's head just beneath the eye. Bending his back as he slices the skin, first above the jaw, then below, he smiles as blood washes over his hands and the shark's massive jaws begin to fall free from its life-less body.

"This killer must be fifteen feet if it's an inch," Charlie says, pausing to wipe the slippery blood from his hands onto his pants. "Bet it weighs half a ton."

"Yeah, it's a monster, all right," Fred agrees, still holding the gaffing hook in the shark's snout.

Sweat pours off Charlie as he cuts through the last bit of gristle that holds the shark's jaws in place. The grisly task complete, Charlie lets the shark slide onto the slippery deck, leaving the skin around its mouth flapping and loose.

"Okay, give me the knife," Fred orders. "That fin could be worth a lot of bucks."

Charlie hands the bloody knife to Fred and starts to clean the bits of skin off the menacing set of jaws. "Some shop on the wharf is going to pay big," he mumbles as he works. Meanwhile, Fred hunches over the cut and bleeding brute and saws the base of its dorsal fin. After several minutes, the blade breaks through the leathery skin on the shark's back and the fin topples onto the deck.

Frank stands, wipes the sweat from his face, and shrugs. "Well, I don't have the stomach for shark-fin soup, but I'm sure glad some people do!" He laughs, then glances down at what remains of the mutilated creature. "That's it for him, Charlie. Let's throw the carcass over the side. Give me a hand."

"In a minute," Charlie replies, concentrating on something he has found while cleaning the set of jaws. "This brute was a killer," he says, shaking his head. "Look what I found wedged in its teeth." He holds up a piece of Styrofoam about the size of his weather-beaten hand.

"What's that?" asks Fred.

"I think it's part of a surfboard. I remember hearing on the shortwave that a board washed up on a beach about thirty miles south of here last week. There was a bite mark in the center—and no surfer."

"Let's cut open the belly and see what else we find," Fred suggests, struggling to turn the huge beast on its back. "These brutes are nothing but eating machines, that's what they are. They never get filled up. One taste of human blood and they go absolutely mad."

The two men stand over the dead shark for a moment, then Fred hands the knife to Charlie. "Why don't you do the honors?" he asks solemnly, then grins.

Charlie grins back. "Why, thank you." And with that, he plunges the knife into the pearly white underside of the creature, just below its now jawless mouth. Yanking the blade toward the shark's tail, he watches expressionless as the beast's skin falls away, revealing its organs. Bending down, Fred reaches into the bloody mass and finds the stomach, then pulls a smaller knife from a sheath on his belt and slices it open. Reaching into the soft tissue, he pulls out several objects—a seal fin, another piece of Styrofoam, and several shreds of rubber from a wet suit.

The two men look at one another with tight-lipped smiles.

"You're right," Charlie says. "These sharks are bloodthirsty. It's a good thing there aren't too many around." He stands and wipes his hands. "In fact, this is the only great white shark I've ever seen."

"Hey, check this out!" Fred exclaims, still feeling his way through the shark's gut. He grunts, moans, and finally pulls a small shark from the gory mess. It is about a three-foot-long miniature great white.

"Don't tell me it eats its own kind, too?" Charlie asks, a look of disbelief on his face.

"Naw," Fred says. "There are no teeth marks on him." He lets out a deep belly laugh. "Looks to me like we caught ourselves a mama shark!" He throws the lifeless baby shark onto the deck. "Come on, let's clean up this mess," he says with a sneer.

The two men grumble and complain as they struggle with the mangled carcass and finally heave it overboard.

"We'll probably make a couple of grand from the jaw and fin alone," Fred observes, watching the bloody mess sink into the ocean depths. He and Charlie stand there for a moment as the blue waters claim back the once-powerful, but now unrecogniz-able beast.

"Yeah, and we got rid of a killer, too," Charlie adds, as he wipes some blood off his brow.

Old Chums

Shannon Webb gagged as she pried the top off the forty-gallon barrel filled with chopped mackerel, mangled grouper, and shredded sea bass. It was *chum*—what fishermen call the bait they use to attract sharks—and the sight of it hit her like a fist to the face. She grabbed a scoop and prepared to toss the stinky mess of bloody fish heads, glittering fish eyes, and oily fish insides over the side of the *Tiburon*. The old fishing boat was chugging along about ten miles south of Pensacola, Florida, in the Gulf of Mexico.

"I thought you liked seafood, Shannon," Reedy, Shannon's boss and the owner of the *Tiburon*, said with a grin.

Shannon held her nose and Reedy let out a barking laugh, then turned back to the wheel. "Better get used to it, young lady," he said from his perch toward the front of the thirty-five-foot boat.

The only part of the vessel that was shielded from the blazing sun, Reedy's perch was under a canvas awning.

Although he was gruff, Shannon had really grown to like Reedy, especially since he had been a close friend of her father's. In fact, Reedy had taken Shannon under his wing ever since Steve Webb, her dad, had died in a scuba-diving accident two years before. The death report had said that Webb's air hose had torn on a jagged piece of metal in an underwater wreck. He'd drowned before anyone could reach him, deep in the sunken hull of the downed ship.

The tragedy had turned Shannon's mother into a recluse, but Shannon had battled grief by spending her free time on the water or around the docks her father had loved. She was built like her dad—tall, lanky, and blond. She also had the same inner strength he had been famous for. Shannon Webb, like Steve Webb, never quit. She wanted to be the best at everything, from swimming to running to algebra. Whatever the task was, she wanted to excel at it—even if it was chumming.

Feeling sorry for Shannon after her father's death, Reedy had hired the teenager to work weekends and vacations in his bait-and-tackle store, the Shark Shack. She stocked supplies, helped customers, filled bait coolers, and cleaned up when Reedy took fishing parties out on the gulf.

"I trust you more than I trust Logan," Reedy had confided to her once, speaking of his business partner. "He's a tough one, that Logan."

Now Logan stood on deck a few feet away from Shannon, baiting steel hooks for two men who had hired the boat and crew for a shark-fishing trip. The men had entered the Gulf Coast catch-and-release shark tournament, and Shannon could tell by the way they talked that they were real amateurs.

She remembered that Reedy hadn't been much concerned with catch-and-release tournaments until the two amateur fishermen had wandered into the Shark Shack. Actually, he had told her on many an occasion before they'd walked in that the whole idea seemed downright strange. "Fish, especially sharks, are for catching and keeping," the old sailor had told Shannon. And, in fact, the walls of the Shark Shack were lined with shark jaws and mounted shark bodies—the result of years of running the best shark-hunting boat on the Gulf Coast.

But business had dropped off, and it was becoming harder and harder to find sharks anywhere. It looked like catch-and-release trips were going to be about the only kind of shark trips Reedy would have to support his shop. "Maybe the sharks are just fished out," Reedy had finally admitted to Shannon one day. "Could be why business has slowed so much."

Reedy had also admitted that the work Shannon's father had been doing before he died—work Reedy had once scoffed at—was important. Steve Webb, an environmentalist, had been in the process of conducting a coastal shark census. Before his life was tragically cut short, he'd planned to push for laws protecting certain sharks under the Endangered Species Act. But with Webb's death, the census work and the push for legislation had stopped.

Today the *Tiburon* was headed to the same sunken freighter where Shannon's father had drowned, several miles farther south and a hundred feet down. The old wreck was home to dozens of species of fish that fed on other species. At the top of the feeders were the sharks. Blues, tigers, hammerheads, white-tips, even makos—they all swarmed around the sunken ship like bees at a hive.

"About ten minutes till we reach the freighter, Shannon. Start throwing the chum overboard to draw the sharks." Reedy's voice rumbled over the throbbing diesel engines.

Shannon looked at the man she had all but allowed to take her father's place. He wasn't old, Shannon figured, about fifty, the same age her father would have been. But years on the ocean had taken its toll, making Reedy's skin tight and leathery, his eyes fixed in a permanent squint. He was certainly a character, with his thick crop of blond hair pulled back into a long, thin braid that had a shiny blue-and-yellow-striped bead dangling at the end.

"Throw your lines over!" Reedy yelled to the sweating men who'd hired him. The amateur fishermen were strapped in heavy wood-and-metal chairs bolted to the floor like barbershop seats. "We'll troll around the freighter and hope the chum draws you some sharks."

Shannon felt a wave of sickness as she dipped the scoop into the bloody shark bait. She loved the ocean, and had lived her whole fifteen years in Pensacola. The gulf breezes, the white beaches, the crying gulls—she loved the whole package. But she *hated* chum. The problem was that chumming was the best way— sometimes the *only* way—to attract sharks. That's why the Shark Shack sold so much of the disgusting stuff to other fishing parties. Shannon could barely make herself go into the store's back room. That's where disgusting bait fish were chopped and tossed into barrels, turning the work area into what looked almost like a slaughterhouse.

As Shannon threw the chum overboard, a strong breeze

kicked bloody spray back into her face, but she didn't stop. She scooped and tossed as fast as she could. The water darkened to a purplish red as the greasy, slick stuff spread out behind the slow-moving boat. Logan stood behind the straw-hatted tourists, waiting to coach them if a shark hit their lines.

"How them fish guts taste, missy?" Logan called to Shannon in his raspy voice.

Shannon smiled good-naturedly, but Logan gave her the creeps. His sense of humor, like Reedy's, left something to be desired. Still, she laughed at his attempt at a joke, determined to prove that she was as good a crew*man* as anyone.

"Delicious, Logan!" she called back. "Want me to save some for your dinner?"

Logan was a short barrel of a man, about Reedy's age. His gray hair grew straight out from the sides of his head like steel wool, leaving a shiny bald lane in the middle. Most of his upper teeth were gone, so his mouth had a caved-in look, and red, zip-perlike scars crisscrossed his arms. He walked with a stiff-legged limp, and no one seemed to know how he got it.

Grinning like a nasty jack-o'-lantern, Logan was about to tease Shannon back, but his reply was cut off by a sharp cry from one of the men strapped in the fishing chair.

"Whoa!" the man whose nickname was Chick yelped. "I-I've got something! Something *big*!

He jackknifed forward, straining against his safety belt as his thick fishing pole bent almost double. Mike, his friend who was strapped into the chair next to him, reeled in his line and moved out of his seat to cheer on his companion's struggle. "Atta way, Chick!" Mike yelled. "Keep that line tight, old man!"

Shannon dropped the scoop into the chum barrel and moved to the starboard to watch the action. She knew that anyone who had hooked a good-sized shark faced a fight that would last a while.

After nearly forty-five minutes of fighting the invisible weight beneath the waves, Chick whooped as an unmistakable triangular fin rose above the foam near the boat. At that point, Logan reached into a storage compartment built into the deck near the stern. He groped through the wrenches, screwdrivers, and hammers until he finally pulled out an evil-looking hook shaped like a question mark that was almost as long as his forearm. Bracing himself, he prepared to sink the sharp tool, called a gaffing hook, into the beast. After that, the grunting tourist would continue to reel his prize closer into the boat, while Logan and Reedy attempted to haul the wounded shark onboard.

"It's a blue shark!" Logan shouted. "Could be six feet!"

Shannon watched in awe as Logan swung the gaff over the side just as the huge shark, a gunmetal blue, turned its white belly upward in a frantic effort to shake free of the barbed hook. Then Logan sank the sharp metal of the gaff into the beast's thick skin just beneath its lower jaw, and with Reedy's help, he hauled the streamlined, cigar-shaped shark out of the water. It flipped onto the slippery deck, and Logan pulled the gaff free, then slid back toward the compartment as the bleeding monster skidded around on the wet wood. Then, without a single shred of fear in his eyes, Logan placed his huge hand on the shark's head to keep it from biting him and roughly ripped the fisherman's still-baited hook from the shark's mouth.

Shannon guessed the shark to be nearly six feet long—the

biggest shark she'd ever seen alive. Its sleek body was as big around as a large tree trunk, and its mouth opened wide enough to take in a man's arm or leg. She could almost feel the pressure of the shark's bite as its jaws snapped shut, and its catlike eyes sent a wave of fear along her spine.

Reedy, his braid dancing in the breeze, handed a tape measure to Shannon, then grabbed the shark's tail and pinned its belly down on the deck. "Grab your camera, Chick," he said to the smiling tourist who'd landed the big fish. "And have your buddy Mike snap a shot of you and this brute." Then he turned to Shannon. "Hurry up and let's measure it. The sooner we let it go, the better."

Suddenly the frantic shark twisted violently. "Keep the head steady, Logan!" Reedy shouted. "And watch your fingers."

The deck was a flurry of action. Shannon bent over and measured the shark, careful to stay clear of its snapping jaws. "Five feet and . . . about . . . ten inches!" she called out. Then she stepped back while Mike took several pictures of Chick kneeling over his thrashing prize.

"All right, everybody stand back," Reedy shouted. "The catch has been verified and I'm going to let this poor beast go." He looked at Logan. "When I step back it'll probably start flipping. You grab the tail and toss him back."

"Right," Logan growled, squinting at his partner in the bright sun.

Shannon never understood why the two men called themselves partners. She thought of partners as friends, and she'd often seen Logan fix Reedy with an angry glare when Reedy ordered him around.

Everyone scrambled out of the way as Logan bent his squat, muscular body beside the shark. Reedy, his work done, led Chick and Mike, who kept high-fiving each other, to the wheelhouse for cold beers. Shannon was thirsty, too, and would have loved a soft drink. But when Logan didn't release the shark right away, she stayed behind to watch.

Suddenly Shannon saw a glint of steel as Logan pulled a jagged knife from a sheath on his belt. He moved his arm rapidly in a sawing motion, and Shannon moved closer, craning her neck over Logan's shoulder to see what he was doing. At that moment, he turned around, holding the shark's bloody triangular dorsal fin in his hairy hand.

His eyes fixed on hers, Logan didn't say a word for a moment, but his look was enough to send a shiver down Shannon's spine. She looked down at the shark, and then her eyes came back to meet Logan's cold gaze.

"Our secret—*right,* missy?" Logan said in a menacing voice as he quickly stuffed the foot-long fin into a small canvas sack by the starboard rail.

Once the fin was hidden, Logan grabbed the flopping shark and heaved it over the side with a grunt. Still speechless, Shannon ran to the edge and watched the shark sink, helpless without a dorsal fin to keep it upright. Then she saw dark shapes far below in the clear green water. They were other sharks zeroing in on the blood that quickly reddened the water from the two-foot hole in the released shark's back.

Like torpedoes the predators came from all directions, shredding their disabled kin into tiny fragments in seconds. Shannon watched in horror as the sharks, in their bloodthirsty frenzy, bit anything that moved, including each other. In seconds, the water became a bloody foam of chum—floating shark scraps left over from the violent slaughter.

The loud splashing drew the other men back to the stern. Their eyes widened in disbelief at the mindless killing a few feet away. Ragged bits of shark bodies rose above the now wine-colored water. Reedy looked at Shannon, whose eyes were turned away from the gore. Then he turned to face Logan.

"What happened?" he asked curtly.

"Shark must have been bleeding from the hook," Logan said, shrugging his shoulders. "There was probably a lot of sharks following the boat. You know how those devils are when they smell blood."

"B-but couldn't it escape?" Mike asked, looking a little green. "It didn't look like it was bleeding *that* much." He turned away from the massacre and shuddered.

"Like I said, doesn't take much blood to draw those killers." Logan's voice was stern and clearly meant *no more questions*.

Shannon sensed that Reedy knew Logan was lying. Still, he said nothing as he made his way back to the wheel, brushing his braid back behind his ear. "Getting late," he called over his shoulder. "We'd better be heading back."

Putting the *Tiburon* into full throttle, Reedy whirled the old boat around the outside of the spreading circle of blood and shark flesh. Shannon found an old crate to sit on for the ride back to the harbor. She closed her eyes and tried to erase the frightening sight of the feeding frenzy from her mind. She also made a silent promise to tell Reedy about Logan's cruel butchery . . . when the time was right.

Back home that evening, Shannon sat at the kitchen table, staring blankly at a family photo on the shelf above the sink. Three smiling people stood on the dock not far from the Shark Shack. Shannon was about twelve in the photo, and her hair stuck out in Pippi Longstocking braids. Her father was there, too. Tan and trim, his wide smile pushing the skin around his eyes into rows of wrinkles, he stood next to Shannon's mom. She was also smiling—something that Shannon had hardly seen in the past three years.

Shannon pushed the macaroni and cheese around on her plate, but she couldn't make herself eat.

"What's the matter, honey?" Mrs. Webb asked. "I thought you'd be starved after a day out on the boat. And I made your favorite dinner."

"Mom, was Dad friends with Logan, too?" Shannon asked, preoccupied with the events of the day. "I mean, did he hang out with both guys when he was young—or just with Reedy?"

Mrs. Webb's eyes filled with tears. Shannon knew that she was forcing her mother to think of all that was painful. But she had to know whether her father, the most respected marine biologist on the Gulf Coast, could have been friends with a cruel man like Logan.

Mrs. Webb sighed and twisted her napkin around her finger. "Well, Shannon, I can't say that I knew all of your dad's friends, because he had so many. He grew up here, you know, and was teaching at the university when I moved down."

"Right," Shannon said impatiently. She'd heard the story of the romance between the hometown marine-biology professor and the New England museum director a hundred times. In fact it was more familiar than a bedtime story. "But was he friends with Logan?"

Lost in thought, Mrs. Webb continued. "Reedy and your dad grew up like brothers. He called him Reedy, not John Reed, like everyone else. They bought a boat together in high school. Then your dad went to college and Reedy was drafted and—"

"I remember Dad saying that Reedy served in Vietnam," Shannon said. "But I don't remember him saying anything about Logan serving, too."

Mrs. Webb seemed to come out of a trance. "Logan? Oh, yes, he's hung around the docks for years, bouncing from job to job. I don't think your dad knew him, but I'm not sure. Frankly, I was always kind of frightened by his appearance."

Shannon didn't say anything. She knew that if she told her mother what she had seen, her job at Reedy's shop would be history. As it was, her mother wasn't crazy about Shannon working on the docks. Now Shannon herself wasn't sure how she felt about working there, either.

"The only thing I know about Logan," Mrs. Webb continued, "is that he was in the war, too. He might have been a SEAL, like Reedy."

"A *seal*?" asked Shannon.

"Yes, the navy's underwater demolition team," explained Mrs. Webb. "They're kind of like underwater army rangers."

Shannon picked at her dinner. She'd forgotten that Reedy was a scuba expert. Her father had kept some of his equipment at

Reedy's store, but after the accident, Reedy had sold everything that had to do with scuba diving. He'd given it up, too.

As she forced herself to eat, Shannon made up her mind to go to the bait shop early the next morning and tell Reedy what she had seen. She also planned to find out more about Logan.

A pink band of light on the horizon announced the coming of another sunny day as Shannon arrived at the Shark Shack. Fishing boats left early, and the bait shop was usually busy at sunup. Most mornings, Reedy had the all-weather radio channel on and a cup of coffee nearby as he filled coolers with every kind of bait from minnows to mackerel.

Today, though, the bare bulb hanging from the ceiling was on, but the front room of the shabby store was empty. Shannon felt a chill as she heard Logan's raspy voice singing off-key in the back. The smell of butchered fish drifted through the shop.

"Reedy?" Shannon called in a shaky voice. "Hey, Reedy? You want me to put mackerel in the cooler?"

"He's not here, missy," Logan said, wiping fish guts and scales on his filthy pants as he stepped through the dark back-room door and into the naked light of the front room. "He's probably still sleeping. Long day yesterday, you know?"

"Sleeping?" Shannon asked in a tone that made it clear she didn't believe Logan. "Reedy doesn't sleep. He's says he's like a shark—in constant motion."

"Well, he ain't here," Logan snapped. "So *I'm* the boss as of right now."

Shannon wanted to tell Logan off, tell him that she took orders only from Reedy, not from some shark-butchering weirdo. But she knew something wasn't right, and she had to know whether Reedy was okay. After all, he was almost like a father to her.

"Stock the coolers up front, missy," Logan ordered, walking back through the doorway. "I'm cutting up fish for chum—lot of boats going out for the catch-and-release contest today."

Shannon worked quickly. There was plenty to do before the sun rose any higher and customers began filtering in. Her first job was to restock fishing line, leaders, hooks, lures, and other supplies on the shelves in the front room. As she worked, Shannon heard hacking and sawing sounds followed by the squishy splash of fish parts plopping into the chum barrels.

Cringing, she finished restocking the shelves and walked behind the cash register to a large double-door refrigerator stacked with plastic buckets of bait. It was her job to put each type of bait into smaller containers in the old soda cooler in front of the cash register so customers could quickly make their selections.

Shannon opened the door and pulled a few buckets of mackerel and bonito from the refrigerator. But as she moved the heavy buckets, her eye was drawn to a blood-stained cardboard box about the size of a small suitcase. It was stuffed far in the back of the stainless steel container, almost as though it had been hidden. She grunted as she pulled out the box. *Thirty-five pounds* was scrawled across the cover.

Kneeling beside the heavy box, Shannon opened it and instantly jumped back as though she had been bitten by a snake. The box was tightly packed with the dorsal fins of at least twenty sharks! All had the same jagged marks that Logan's knife had left on the blue shark's dorsal fin the day before. Some looked freshly cut; others smelled rotten, as if they had been kept in the box for months.

"Lookin' for something, missy?"

Shannon screamed at the sound of Logan's voice. He stood in the doorway behind her. She turned to face him and the same cold-eyed stare she'd seen the day before.

"Put 'em back," Logan said in his raspy voice. "They're mine." He laughed huskily. "Then come give me a hand getting the barrels of chum onto the truck outside. I've got to drive them over to the fishing boats."

"N-no. I-I think I'd better stay . . ." Shannon stammered.

"I said *give me a hand!*" Logan growled.

"But what about Reedy?" Shannon said. Her voice was shaking and she was clearly frightened.

"I told you—Reedy's sleeping."

Logan turned toward the back room. Shannon covered the box and shoved it back into the refrigerator. Then she followed Logan into the smelly room filled with knives, cleavers, and saws. A worktable was covered with blood, fish insides, and scales. Beside the table were two covered garbage-can-sized barrels filled with chum.

"I'll back the truck to the door," Logan said. "You slide the barrels onto the step. They're heavy, but the floor's pretty slick." He laughed eerily. "Shouldn't be too hard for a strong young girl like you."

Shannon made her way across the dimly lit room, hoping Reedy would walk through the door. She had to tell him about the fins, about how Logan had caused the feeding frenzy. She wasn't certain that Reedy would do anything, but somehow she knew he needed to know.

Grasping the handles on either side of the first container of chum, Shannon tilted it on its edge and twisted it back and forth while she tugged it toward the door. Because her back was turned, she couldn't see anything in her path, and she never even had a glimpse of the fishtail that had fallen to the floor.

"Aaah!" she screamed as her foot slid on the slippery tail. Falling straight back, she pulled the chum barrel over on top of her, and the weight of the chopped fish pushed the lid off. To her horror, the bloody mess splashed out, covering her legs with heads, eyes, tails, bones, and intestines.

Clamping her hand over her mouth to hold back her breakfast, Shannon gagged. Then, suddenly, her eye was caught by a strange glimmer in the bloody pile of fish guts sprawled all over the place. It wasn't the silvery shimmer of fish scales—it was darker than that. Shannon scrambled to her knees and reached into the goo, pulling out a bead . . . a blue-and-yellow-striped bead—a bead exactly like the one on Reedy's braid!

"REEDY! REEDY!" Shannon screamed. At the bottom of the barrel were bloody clumps of blond hair and bone too thick to have come from chum fish. She opened her mouth to scream again, but before she could, a thick, hairy hand clamped over it.

The *Tiburon* bounced across the waves like a skipping stone. Shaded by the canvas awning, Logan stood at the wheel, staring silently at the horizon as he ran the old boat at full throttle. Shannon sat on deck with her hands tied behind her back and around one of the metal poles that supported the awning.

"The sharks are going to eat well today, eh, missy?" Logan shouted over the engine's roar. He grinned his empty-tooth smile.

"Y-you killed Reedy!" Shannon shouted. She was so angry she could hardly feel her fear.

Logan slowed the boat. They were nearing the sunken freighter. He set the cruise control and hobbled back to the stern railing where the chum barrels were tied. He'd wrestled the barrels onto the truck and from there onto the boat by himself while Shannon was tied and gagged. Once they were out on the gulf where no one could hear her scream, Logan had removed the gag and tied her to a pole that was connected to the starboard rail.

"Yes, missy. I killed him. Partner or not—no one takes money from Harry Logan."

"Money?" Shannon asked.

"Yeah, I get a hundred dollars a pound for those nasty shark fins. People eat 'em in soup." Logan steadied himself by the barrels and removed the top of one. "Reedy and me used to make a fortune before those do-gooders began making noise about sharks dying out."

"But they *are* dying out, Logan!" Shannon said. "That's why your business has been slow. And that's what my fath—"

"Your father turned Reedy against me!" Logan said with a sneer. "Before he butted in, Reedy took the fins and gave them to me to sell. It's not against the law, you know."

"I know. That's what my father was working to change until he died." Shannon hung her head. Suddenly she was

51

overwhelmed by the grief of her father's death and the fear that her own might be near.

"Correction, missy: until Reedy killed him." Logan sneered again as he dipped a large ladle into the chum and threw it behind the boat.

"You're crazy, Logan!" Shannon yelled. "Reedy and my dad were best friends. They grew up together."

Logan laughed. "Oh, sure. Until your rich father went to college, and poor Reedy had to go to Vietnam. That's where I met him. We were divers together." Logan threw more chum overboard. "Reedy owed me his life."

"Wh-what are you talking about?"

"We were on a secret mission in Haiphong harbor. Demolition—setting underwater time bombs on Vietnamese patrol boats. We were down about fifty feet and Reedy didn't see the bull shark coming up on him from behind. Must have been eight feet long."

Logan faced Shannon and pulled his greasy T-shirt up over his belly and chest. Scars ran like highways around his torso. "See these scars? I got them when I distracted the beast so Reedy could set the charges. Shook me like a doll, the shark did. Then spit me out when I stabbed him behind the nose." Logan shook his head. "I nearly bled to death. Got eight hundred stitches. My whole kneecap was torn off."

Shannon turned her face away from the disgusting pink scars. "I don't care what you say. Reedy didn't kill my father."

Logan grinned and turned back to his work. "Well, not exactly. Let's just say that the air hose that ripped open was a little, uh, *worn*."

Shannon strained against the ropes behind her back. "You're a liar, Logan! And you're a fool if you—*aaak!*"

Logan laughed as the ladleful of chum hit Shannon in the face. "A fool, eh? A liar? Listen here, missy. Reedy and your father may have been close, but Reedy knew he had a good thing going with his shark hunts." Logan turned away from Shannon and continued throwing the chum over the stern. "Reedy was making good money. He didn't like your know-it-all father talking down to him about endangered species and the like. And when he saw how much clout your father had with the legislature, he knew that a new law wouldn't be long in coming."

"So? That doesn't mean Reedy killed him," Shannon said, still moving her arms up and down to loosen the rope, stopping each time Logan turned back to dip his ladle into the chum. Suddenly, in her struggling, her hands brushed a stiff cloth leaning against the chair. It felt like canvas. Even though she could not see it, Shannon was almost positive that it was the bag Logan had hidden the fin in yesterday.

"No? Well, I saw Reedy rubbing the air hose he gave to your father with a fin from a mako shark. You know what that's like?"

Shannon hung her head. She knew that a shark's fin was coarse and had sharp edges like tiny teeth on it. In fact, it could cut like a file, shredding just about anything including human flesh—*or a rope!* Shannon's heart leaped with the faint hope that she might have a chance against the evil killer a few feet away. Her hands trembled as she clumsily tried to open the canvas sack. *Please let the fin be there!* her mind cried. *Please!*

Logan continued his rhythmic scooping and tossing, unaware of Shannon's movements. One barrel was just about emptied, and he opened the other. "He made the hose paper thin, Reedy did. Then I saw him switch the hoses on your father's tanks. You know how much pressure there is a hundred feet down, missy?" Logan's eyebrows rose.

"You're lying!" Shannon shouted. But her anger only masked her relief as she felt the sandpapery skin and pointed tip of a dorsal fin. With a dexterity driven by panic, she slipped the fin from the bag and clamped it between her sweaty hands. Watching Logan carefully and timing her motions against his, Shannon carefully moved the fin in a sawing motion across the knotted fibers that bound her hands.

Logan tossed more chum overboard. "Reedy didn't think anyone was watching—but *I* was! Then he owed me his life—*twice.*" Logan laughed. "After your old man died, I threatened to go to the cops unless Reedy cut me in on his business. It was a gold mine—until the last year or so."

"I don't believe a thing you're saying," Shannon said, working the fin up and down and feeling the tight rope loosen with each stroke. "Reedy and my father were best friends."

"*Were,* missy!" Logan snarled, as he dropped the ladle into the chum. Then he knelt and pulled open the top of the tool compartment near the stern. He grabbed a wrench and eyed the bolts holding the fishing chair to the deck. "Reedy wanted your father dead. He only took you under his wing out of guilt. Then he began getting the same fool ideas your father had. When he wouldn't let me take the fin off the boat yesterday, that did it. I snuck back to the shop late last night and 'surprised' him."

Shannon prayed that Logan would not suddenly begin to look for the fin now that he had mentioned it. But the horrible man seemed to have other things on his mind as he knelt by one of the fishing chairs and began to loosen the bolts that fastened it to the deck.

"What are you doing?" Shannon asked as she felt the rope drop free behind her.

"I'm not taking any chances, missy," Logan growled. "I'm tying you to this chair. That way, if the sharks don't get you, the chair will pull you all the way down to the bottom. You'd like to join your father, now, wouldn't you?" Logan chuckled at his cruel joke, then squinted over the stern. "I see a good-sized fin appearing. Why, if someone hooked that monster, it could pull a chair overboard. Sounds like a good story to tell the authorities, right?"

Logan grunted as he loosened the bolts. Shannon knew that it was only a matter of seconds before he would free the chair and tie her to it. And she knew that there was only one way to stay out of the chum-slick waters.

Trying to judge the distance between her and Logan as he continued to unscrew the metal bolts, Shannon tried to work up her courage to jump him while her fear tried to talk her out of it. *Can I jump that far?* she wondered. *And if I get the drop on him—then what?*

Suddenly Shannon knew there was no more time to wonder. Logan had gotten the chair loose from its moorings and he stood up, facing Shannon with an evil grin spreading across his face. He stepped toward her. "Now all I have to do is tie you to the chair and you'll be dead weight, if not food for—"

In a flash, Shannon brought the shark fin from behind her back and exploded upward with the tip of the fin leading the way. Surprised, Logan didn't quite comprehend what was happening until the sharp fin hit him in the Adam's apple, puncturing the soft skin on the top of his windpipe. He staggered backward, gagging and clutching his throat. Then, because the force of Shannon's blow made it impossible for him to keep his balance, Logan toppled over backward and fell to the deck.

But not for long. "Why, you little . . ." he snarled as he scrambled upright and pulled his long knife out from the leather sheaf on his belt.

Shannon knew that her only advantage was to keep moving. Logan was too hobbled and too hurt to catch her—at least for a while. Holding the fin in front of her like a weapon to keep him away, she moved along the edge of the boat toward the stern.

Logan moved toward her unsteadily, the jagged knife extended in front of him, coughing and gagging from the puncture wound in his throat. Dancing around the remaining upright fishing chair, the two enemies eyed each other, each waiting for the other to make a mistake.

Shannon backed toward the stern, near the chum barrels, keeping the chair between herself and Logan. As she stepped back slowly, she glanced for a split second into the tool compartment near her feet. Among the tools, she saw something that could give her a slight edge over her opponent.

Tossing the fin aside, she quickly knelt down and reached among the tools. Her motion drew Logan into an instant charge and he didn't see what Shannon had grabbed.

Exploding from her crouched position, Shannon swung the gaffing hook she now held tightly in her hand in a wide arc. Then, as Logan fell upon her, she dug the curved metal hook into his back. Stunned, he dropped his knife, then looked at her in disbelief.

Gripping the handle with both hands, Shannon pulled Logan down to the deck. Then, with a strength she didn't know she had, she forced his face into a full barrel of chum, holding it there as he struggled to breathe, hoping that the powerful man would somehow black out.

But Shannon had underestimated Logan's strength. He fought wildly, and her grip on the hook loosened as he yanked his head back out of the chum with the superhuman strength a drowning man uses to survive. Like a monster, his blood- and fish-covered body rose up from the barrel, the gaffing hook still in his back. Sputtering, staring at Shannon with hatred, Logan suddenly stumbled backward and tumbled over the stern railing.

Shannon put her hands to her mouth in horror as she saw fins instantly zeroing in on the flailing, screaming Logan. Blood sprayed from the wound in his back like water from a lawn sprinkler as shark after shark struck their helpless prey, spinning him in circles like a bloody top. And then, his toothless mouth forming a black O, he sunk like garbage down a disposal.

Shannon stared at the bloody water behind the boat for several minutes after Logan vanished. She was too stunned and too exhausted to comprehend the events of the past twenty-four hours. A man whose cruelty had sickened her was dead. A man whose kindness had misled her was also dead. And her life had been saved by the same object that had inadvertently caused her father's death—a fin from one of the victim sharks killed by the most bloodthirsty of killers: man.

Her head spinning with confusion, Shannon moved shakily toward the wheel, but stopped and turned back to the stern. Her gaze fell on the smelly barrels of chum, now almost empty. She promised herself that she would never come anywhere near that horrid slop again . . . as soon as she did one more thing.

With a grunt she lifted one barrel onto the railing and emptied it into the water. At the bottom of the barrel she saw a tuft of blond hair and tossed it into the gulf waters. Then she hoisted the other barrel of chum to the railing and did the same thing. The water began to churn as the frenzied sharks tore at the barrels and each other.

"Say hi to your old chum, Logan," Shannon said, then made her way back to the wheel of the *Tiburon*.

Perilous Pool Party

Philip Huckabee looked up from the book he was reading and grinned at his twin brother. "Hey, Peter, listen to this. The bull shark is responsible for more attacks on humans than any other shark in the world."

Peter turned back from the window of the small Lear Jet and yanked the book his brother had been reading right out of his hands. "Bull shark? That's bull! The great white kills more people than any other shark!"

Philip grabbed the book back and gave his brother a hard shove. "Wrong!" he said in his know-it-all voice. "Read this!" He pointed to a page in the book, then slammed it shut. "Oh, I forgot. You can't read, can you, *Petey*?"

Mr. and Mrs. Huckabee rolled their eyes and sighed. The long trip from Dallas to Australia had been dreadful, and this charter flight from Sydney to the exclusive Crater Island resort was a nightmare. The twins were getting on each other's nerves and on the nerves of the other passengers, who'd had enough of the boys' constant pinching, poking, and teasing of one another.

Peter punched his brother on the arm, then grabbed Philip's book again. He quickly flipped to the section on bull sharks. *"Bull sharks are dark brown on top, with black-tipped fins,"* he read aloud. *"The shark gets its name from the hump behind its head. Bull sharks grow to an adult length of approximately eight feet and may weigh 600 pounds or more."*

"Cool!" Philip exclaimed, leaning over his brother's shoulder. He pointed at the picture of the deadly creature. "Pretty scary, huh?"

By way of an answer, Peter slammed the book shut on his twin's finger and looked out his window.

"Ow!" Philip yelped.

But Peter just ignored his brother. Far below, the Coral Sea spread out like a giant blue cloth, broken only by drifting wisps of clouds. There was a sudden whine as the jet's engines were throttled back and the sleek plane descended toward the vast ocean below. Peter, Philip, and their parents were headed for a two-week vacation on Crater Island, thirty miles off the coast of Queensland, Australia.

"Hey, I see the island," said Peter, pressing his nose against the glass. "From up here, it looks like a huge comma."

Mr. and Mrs. Huckabee looked out their own window. Sure enough, Peter's description was right. The island was a green curve in the sky-blue water, with a round rise at the northern end formed by a relatively small, long-extinct volcano. As they flew over the glorious sight, the captain's voice came over the intercom and explained that the mouth of the volcano had collapsed into a huge bowl, and the crater formed by the collapse gave the island its name.

As the jet soared closer to their destination, the inner curve of the green comma appeared white, marking the shimmering sands of the beaches on the island.

"It's beautiful," Mrs. Huckabee murmured. Then she nudged her husband and pointed to a gleaming white structure shaped like a huge cereal box built inside the slope of the crater at the northern end of the island.

Mr. Huckabee peered closely out the window as the plane sank through the wispy clouds. "I believe you're right," he said, as the plane turned toward the flat south end of the island and headed for a short strip of black asphalt that served as a runway. "And see that blue star shape actually built into the bottom of the crater? That's the five-acre pool the brochure referred to."

"It's magnificent!" Mrs. Huckabee declared. "It looks like the bottom of a teacup."

While their parents continued to gaze at the island far below, the twins had finally settled down a little bit. While Peter had his face pressed against the jet's window, Philip had grabbed his book back and was reading silently.

Bull sharks have a habit of swimming close to shore and have attacked bathers in less than four feet of water. Philip's eyes widened as he read on. *In 1982, on Crater Island off the coast of Australia, thirteen-year-old Gary Warner was wading in water about four feet deep when he was suddenly jolted by something. Terrified, the boy looked down and, to his horror, saw that the clear*

61

water had begun to redden. A split second later, young Warner was catapulted out of the water by an unseen force, blood spraying from severed arteries no longer attached to his leg.

"Awesome!" Philip said out loud, hoping to get Peter's attention away from the window. It worked.

"What's awesome?" Peter asked nonchalantly.

Philip grinned and told his brother about Gary Warner, then read out loud: *"Witnesses said that they saw a brown shark with a huge hump on its back rise from the water and pull Warner under. By the time rescuers dragged the youth to the beach, his right buttock and the flesh down his right leg to the knee were completely torn away. The thigh bone was laid bare and dark red blood gushed uncontrollably from the severed femoral artery. Warner bled to death in minutes."*

"Excellent!" Peter exclaimed. "You'd better keep an eye on your, um, *buttock* when you go wading! It's a pretty big target!" He burst out laughing and turned back to watch the ocean pass below.

Stung, Philip elbowed his brother and was promptly elbowed back. Then the boys began shoving and grunting, their fat cheeks reddening as they fought.

"Boys! Stop it!" Mrs. Huckabee screeched, turning around in her seat to glare over the top at her constantly squabbling sons.

"Yeah, knock it off!" Mr. Huckabee growled, looking away from the window. "This is my vacation, too. Not to mention everyone else's on the plane."

The twins sank sullenly into their seats, ignoring the icy stares focused on them from the other passengers. Embarrassed by their children's behavior, Mr. and Mrs. Huckabee buried their heads in magazines and tried to tune out the mumbled comments drifting down the aisle over the drone of the engines.

What's wrong with the parents?

If they were my kids, I'd . . .

Two weeks on an island with those monsters?!

Peter and Philip looked at each other and smiled. They weren't just identical in their mischievous behavior, they were impossible to tell apart. Both had their father's thick brown curls and their mother's square chin. Their eyebrows, noses, and even their freckle placement matched exactly, and each had rolls of fat around his middle, with no more than a pound separating them. Even their voices were identical, sounding so much alike that their parents couldn't tell who was speaking without looking.

Other traits also marked the rambunctious brothers as twins. Peter was left-handed and Philip right-handed, making one perfect for playing first base and the other a natural at third. When Peter lost a tooth on the left side of his mouth, Philip lost the same tooth on the right side—*on the same day*. It was eerie. It was uncanny . . . and the twins used it to their advantage to drive their parents and everyone else crazy.

As the plane began its final approach to the runway, the engines' whine grew more piercing, filling the cabin. Philip glanced over at Peter and winked, then cupped his hands around his mouth and bellowed: "Oh, no! I see white smoke! White smoke is coming from the engine! We're gonna die!"

People gasped and strained to look back at the tail-mounted engine. Small children began to whimper. The flight attendant scurried down the aisle, reassuring people.

Mrs. Huckabee didn't bother to look out the window. She

spun in her seat and looked back at the twins, uncertain which one to scold. As it became clear that the shout had been a joke, faces glared angrily at both her and her sons.

"That's it, boys," she said, her face reddening. "When we get to the resort, you have to stay in the suite—for two hours!"

"Two hours!" Peter yelled. "Why me? I didn't do anything! It was Philip."

"No, it wasn't!" Philip shouted. "It was Peter!"

Mr. Huckabee unbuckled his seat belt and stood up, his face a twisted mask of anger. "Look, fellas. If you don't straighten out, you'll be in the room all day!" He slumped back into his seat, refastened his seat belt, and scowled until the plane touched down, not saying a single word.

The twins, however, did anything but scowl. They knew that neither their father nor their mother would enforce their threats of discipline. They always made a big show of toughness in front of other people, but the reality of it was that Peter and Philip usually got away with murder.

Banished to the room for what had ended up being a three-hour punishment, the twins had already nearly destroyed their lavish surroundings. Now Philip was bouncing up and down on the paisley sofa, his belly shaking as each jump lifted him higher. Growing bored with that, he leaped over the coffee table to the overstuffed emerald-green chair. But as he landed on the chair, he lost his balance and knocked over a lamp, sending it crashing to the floor. After studying the shattered porcelain and realizing he'd better get the mess cleaned up before his parents returned from playing tennis, he dialed the front desk.

"Um . . . there's been an accident in suite 1404," he said innocently into the phone. "A lamp fell off a table. Can you send someone to clean it up?" He looked at the digital watch on his left wrist. "In the next half hour?" That was how much time he and Peter had left of their punishment. It was a compromise that had almost gotten whittled down to nothing, but then Peter had to go and trip some old lady in the baggage-claim area.

"Wonderful!" Philip said, trying to sound like a grown-up. "Then I'll be waiting for the replacement." He thanked the person on the other end of the line and hung up.

Ignoring his brother, Peter stood on the balcony, gazing down at the enormous star-shaped saltwater pool covering almost the entire floor of the crater. He'd overheard the bellhop say it was bigger than a football field.

Actually, what Peter was looking into was the large circular pool at the center of five smaller pools set around it. Those pools were triangular and served as each of five points in a gigantic star. The sections were different depths—some were as shallow as three feet, others were as deep as fifteen. They were all linked by walkways and footbridges, and gathered around them were, from Peter's point of view, ant-sized people lying on colorful towels or clustered under umbrellas that looked like striped mushrooms.

Peter had a fantastic view of the whole crater in which the enormous pool was set. From fourteen floors up, his gaze traveled to the far side of the star-shaped pool, where he saw a wide stone stairway leading up to the top of the crater, where a concrete courtyard was spread out. A few tourists who had climbed to the top of this stairway from the pool area were walking along the courtyard, which faced the southern portion of the island and overlooked the bay.

Peter looked at what those tourists in the courtyard were probably looking at—puffs of surf crashing onto an untouched white beach that bordered the bay's turquoise water. *Why isn't anybody on the beach?* Peter wondered, unable to make out any lifeguard chairs or brightly colored beach umbrellas in the distance. *It's stupid to fly all the way to Australia to swim in a pool, no matter how big it is.*

He looked at the digital watch that pinched his right wrist and smiled at how serious his parents had been about the "sentence" they'd so solemnly delivered. It was already 3:15, and with only fifteen minutes of the sentence left to serve, Peter decided to get into his swimming trunks and check out the beach nobody was exploring.

Actually, three hours alone in a fancy hotel room really wasn't much of a punishment for the twins. They spent most of their days at home alone anyway, supervised by a nanny, a gardener, and a cook. They'd eat snacks, bounce around on the furniture, watch TV, or play video games in much the same way they were doing here at the hotel. Mr. Huckabee's oil drilling business kept him traveling most of the week and Mrs. Huckabee was a lawyer who spent endless hours at the office. So spending hours entertaining themselves in plush surroundings with every toy they could possibly want was old news to the Huckabee twins.

There was a knock on the suite door. As Peter disappeared into the bedroom to change into his trunks, Philip let in a young,

66

dark-haired maid wearing a gray uniform who had come to clean up his mess. Her plastic nameplate read LAURA. She looked at the broken lamp, then at Philip, and shook her head.

"That's a thousand-dollar lamp, *sir*," she said, almost choking on the last word.

Philip stared at the broken porcelain. "It happened by accident. Something shook the table. I think someone in the room below was—"

Seeing the maid was wise to him, Philip stopped in midsentence. "Look, my parents will pay for it," he said with a sneer. "Just put it on the bill. Oh, and could you please hurry, uh, *Laura*?" he asked, inflecting her name with the same tone she'd used for *sir*. "My parents will be back in about—" he checked the watch on his left wrist "—four minutes." And with that he turned and walked briskly into the bedroom to change into swimming trunks that identically matched his brother's.

Her cheeks reddening, Laura yanked a broom and dustpan off her cart. She turned around just as Peter walked into the living room, tying his trunks. He looked at her, then at the lamp, then at his watch.

"You little brat!" shouted Laura, doing a double take, for the boy certainly had returned fast—and changed clothes, too! "I ought to spank you with this broom. What makes you think you can treat me like—"

"What are you yelling at me for, lady?" Peter asked, a quizzical look on his face. "I didn't knock the lamp over."

"Of course not," Laura snapped, stooping to pick up the large pieces of porcelain before sweeping up the shards. "And I'm the Queen of England."

"No, really. I didn't do it. My—"

"Do what?" Mrs. Huckabee asked, stepping through the open door and tossing her tennis racket onto the couch. As she plopped down onto the plush piece of furniture to remove her sneakers, she saw the broken lamp on the far side of the chair. "Okay, who did it?"

"Philip was jumping on the furniture," Peter said matter-of-factly. "Can we go to the beach, Mother? We've been cooped up all day."

Laura did a second double take as Philip walked out of the bedroom and stood next to his brother. He looked at the lamp and shook his head. "Peter, I told you to quit jumping on the furniture," he said in a serious tone. "Now look what you've done. That lamp probably cost a thousand dollars. How could you do this to Mother and Daddy?"

"Me?" Peter fumed. "*I* didn't do it!"

"Do what?" Mr. Huckabee stepped into the room and looked around suspiciously. "You guys weren't causing a ruckus again, were you?" He looked at the maid, then at the pile of broken porcelain at her feet.

"A lamp fell, sir," Laura said, kneeling to sweep the pieces into a dustpan. "Your son—I'm not sure which one—gave approval for me to put the cost of replacing it on the bill."

Mrs. Huckabee sighed and gazed forlornly out the window, while Mr. Huckabee scratched his head and tried to appear calm.

"Look here, boys," he said. "Your mother and I work very hard, and we *need* a vacation. Things'll go a whole lot better if you two stay out of trouble." He paused for a moment as if thinking. "And if you don't, I'll put you on the next plane back to Dallas."

"Daddy?" Philip said, yawning. "Can we go to the beach now?"

"We promise not to get into trouble if you let us go body surfing and stuff," Peter added innocently.

Laura looked up from her work. "Beg your pardon, folks. But no one swims in the bay this time of the year. It's too dangerous."

"Dangerous?" Peter asked, his curiosity aroused. "You mean because of sharks?"

"Sharks? No, not really," Laura answered. "I mean, they're always around, but they usually stay at the mouth of the bay. No, the real danger at the beach is the sea wasps."

Philip wrinkled his forehead. "The *what*?"

"Sea wasps," Laura repeated. "Poisonous jellyfish. The current carries them inshore every year between December and March. A sting from one can kill you in a few minutes."

"So that's why everyone stays at the pool," Peter said, disappointed. "How boring."

"Not really," Laura said. "The hotel plans plenty of fun activities around the pool. In fact, the day after tomorrow there's going to be a big pool party." Noticing that the chubby twins were unimpressed, she added, "There'll be more seafood than you can possibly eat. We'll have sky divers and a magician. And some of us on the staff will entertain."

"Bo-*ring*!" Philip said, rolling his eyes. "Party, schmarty—who wants to sit around a stupid old pool? There's nothing to do but swim and sweat." And then he threw a wicked grin at Peter, who winked back. They quickly whispered something back and forth into each other's ear, then looked at Laura.

"The party sounds like a lot of fun," Philip said, still grinning.

"Yeah," Peter agreed. "We're there!"

Mr. and Mrs. Huckabee just looked at each other and then at their boys. Obviously the bratty little monsters were cooking up something.

The next day, Mr. and Mrs. Huckabee had a tennis lesson scheduled at noon, so the boys ate lunch by the pool. Already bored by the lack of anything to do but squirt his brother with sunscreen, Philip pushed away his half-eaten cheeseburger and grabbed a fistful of crushed ice from his orange soda. Hiding the ice behind him, he caught Peter's eye and nodded toward Laura. Staff members at the hotel were allowed to use the pool during their off-hours, and Laura was lying facedown on a lounge chair. Now she would be Philip's next victim.

Sliding off his chair, he crept over to Laura, who was breathing deeply as if sleeping. When he was directly over her, Philip grinned devilishly and dropped his fistful of slushy ice smack between her shoulder blades.

"AAH! AAAAH!" Laura screamed, flipping over, but not in time to see Philip dash up the long concrete stairway that led to the bay overlook. Instead, she focused her angry gaze on Peter, who sat in his chair a few feet away, shaking with laughter.

"You little twit!" Laura shouted, too upset to care whether she was heard yelling at a guest. "If I was your mother, I'd thrash you within an inch—"

"I didn't *do* anything," Peter said defiantly. "You keep blaming me for stuff that my brother does." He pointed up the steep stairway to Philip, whose belly jiggled as he laughed hysterically.

Laura grabbed her towel and left, muttering under her breath. As she walked over a wooden footbridge leading back to the main building, she stopped and turned around. "I've got a good mind to tell your folks not to bring you to the pool party," she yelled, shaking her fist at the brothers.

Peter ignored Laura and puffed his way up the long stairway to join Philip, now gazing toward the distant beaches below. The cement overlook they stood on was built atop a shrub-covered hill that sloped down to the bay. Several benches were set up on the overlook near viewing binoculars aimed toward the sparkling turquoise water. Philip stepped up to the large binoculars and gazed through them. As he moved the binoculars slowly back and forth on the swivel stand, Peter breathed over his shoulder, waiting impatiently for his turn.

Suddenly Philip stopped. "Hey, I think I see something!"

Peter rolled his eyes. "Well, duh! That's what the binoculars are for!"

"No, doofus, I mean something under the water—like close to the surface!" Philip's excitement aroused Peter's interest. He pushed Philip away and looked through the powerful lenses.

"See the dark shapes in the water—right down at the bottom of the hill?" Philip asked.

"Yeah . . . yeah, I think so. They're long and oval—like giant footballs. What are they? Big rocks?" Peter asked as he slowly moved the binoculars. Suddenly he pulled away from the binoculars and looked at his brother. "Hey, I saw them move!"

"I bet they're sharks!" Philip exclaimed. "Laura said they're always at the mouth of the bay. Remember?"

"Yeah!" Peter exclaimed. "Let's go get a closer look!"

71

A sign posted on the iron railing running around the overlook warned AUTHORIZED PERSONS ONLY BEYOND THIS POINT! As if the sign weren't even there, the twins squeezed through the railing and alternately ran and slid down the outside slope of the crater leading away from the hotel. For several minutes they made their way downhill along a trail cut through low-growing tropical shrubs; then Philip, who was leading the way, stopped short and held his arm out to stop Peter.

The slope ended and dropped off abruptly at an enormous concrete wall that looked like a freeway overpass. As he peered over the edge of the concrete, Philip saw a large circular metal pipe poking out at the base of the wall just a few feet above the clear water.

"Look at that," Philip said, pointing down to the large pipe. "I'll bet it leads back to the pool."

"Want to climb down and follow it back?" Peter asked, sweat running down his cheeks.

Before Philip could answer, both boys heard a strange humming as some kind of motor kicked on. Then, from the pipe below their feet, a loud splash signaled the release of a torrent of water that gushed out into the blue bay.

"I told you," Philip said. "That pipe is probably part of the pool drain."

"I wonder how it works," Peter said as the water slowly tapered off and then abruptly came to a stop.

Suddenly a stocky, red-haired man with a lined, weather-beaten face came crashing through the brush and up to the boys. He wore a baseball cap and grease-stained coveralls with NILES sewn across the pocket.

In the brush behind the man, the boys caught a glimpse of a large gray metal box about three feet square that looked like the circuit-breaker box in their basement at home. A door on the box was open, revealing a bank of switches and a large red lever. The box was attached to a metal pole sunk into the cement at the edge of the wall.

"You kids ain't supposed to be down here. Didn't you see the sign?" the man growled, then narrowed his eyes as he looked from Philip to Peter. "You're the Huckabees, aren't you?"

Peter and Philip looked at each other and grinned. Their reputation was spreading.

"I'm Peter," said Philip.

"I'm Philip," said Peter.

"I'm Niles, head of maintenance, and neither of you lads belongs here." He shook his hand. "You're lucky you didn't fall into the water."

The boys followed his glance toward the water, about ten feet below.

"Low tide, like now, the water's only five feet deep," Niles said. "Break your neck if you tumbled in."

"What about high tide?" Peter wanted to know.

"Comes nearly to the top of the wall," Niles said matter-of-factly. "And comes in fast, too."

"It's not so dangerous at that time, right?" Philip asked.

Niles shrugged. "Not if you can swim. Trouble is, there are a few beasties in the water that are none too friendly."

"Sea wasps?" asked Peter.

"Them, too. But I was talking about sharks—at least out here at the north end of the bay." Niles squinted toward the water.

"Matter of fact . . ." He stopped and pointed at several dark shapes out about twenty yards. "There's some of our razor-toothed friends right there."

"I *knew* they were sharks!" Peter cried, his voice rising.

"We saw them through the binoculars," Philip explained, pointing back up to the walkway. "What kind are they?"

"Bulls, probably," Niles said. "They wait for schools of fish that travel across the mouth of the bay, then chase them into the shallows to feed."

As if on cue, there was a sudden thrashing in the shallow water as several sharks converged on a school of fish that had wandered too close. The boys watched in open-mouthed awe as more and more large shapes gathered to feed only twenty yards from where they stood.

Philip looked into the distance at the curving white sand running around the bay. "Do they ever go toward the beach?"

Niles shook his head. "Even sharks stay away from the sea wasps," he said. "Besides, as you can see, there's plenty of food out here. Now, come on, fellas. Enough talk. Let's get back before I lose my job." Niles began to climb up the hill.

As the twins followed behind, Philip looked over toward the metal box and saw that Niles had left the door open. He poked Peter and nodded toward the electrical switches that were in plain sight. Their eyes met, and in that special twin telepathy they shared, each understood what their next stunt would be.

"Where does that pipe go?" Philip asked innocently, as the trio reached the overlook and paused to catch their breath.

Niles pulled off his cap and wiped the sweat from his fore-head. "Pipe? You mean the drain. It goes to a filter."

Peter tried to get Philip's attention, to signal him that he'd better not ask too many questions or Niles might remember that he'd left the door open. But Philip ignored his brother and barged ahead, his curiosity getting the better of him.

"Filter?" Philip asked. "Where?"

"There's a six-foot square door at the bottom of the central pool. Below it is a huge tank that cleans and circulates all the water. You know, to make sure it doesn't get too salty or dirty. I open it every—" Suddenly he slapped his forehead. "Wait a minute! Did I forget to lock the pump case?"

Aware that his curiosity might have ended their prank, Philip looked at Peter and slapped his own forehead. The boys exchanged disappointed glances as Niles began to climb back through the railing to close the circuit box.

But just after the man had taken a few steps back down the hill, the static-filled crackle of a loudspeaker echoed across the pool area.

"Niles O'Mara . . . Please report to the manager's office. Niles, please report immediately!"

Niles stopped and thrust his hands deep into his coveralls. His face turned redder than it already was, and the boys could sense that he was angry.

"Niles this, Niles that!" he grumbled, as he walked past the boys toward the stairs. "I've got half a mind to tell them what they can do with their hotel."

Peter and Philip watched Niles hustle down the stairs, muttering under his breath. They grinned at each other evilly, overjoyed that the handyman had gotten distracted from his task. "Cool!" they whispered in unison, both thinking the same thing.

"See you later, Niles!" Philip called.

"Yeah, it was nice to meet you!" Peter added.

"Good to meet you, too, boys," Niles yelled over his shoulder. Then he stopped short and turned around. "Now, you boys don't get into any mischief—you hear me?"

"We won't!" the boys lied.

Philip crept over to his brother's bed in the dark and shook him. "Peter," he whispered. "Peter, wake up!"

"Whaaa . . . huh?" Peter rubbed his eyes, still half asleep.

"It's three o'clock," Philip whispered excitedly. "Let's go!"

Peter sat up groggily and pressed the light on his watch. "Did you check outside?" he asked, nodding toward the window that overlooked the pool. A full moon hung high above the island, bathing the land in a pearly white glow.

"Yeah, nobody's down there," said Philip. "Hurry up and get dressed." He reached under his bed and pulled out a small flashlight. "We've got work to do."

The boys sneaked past their snoring parents' room and slipped into the hallway. Then they hustled down the fire escape stairwell and made their way out to the pool, hiding in shadows so no one would see them. Sneaking along footbridges that linked the different sections, the two boys finally made it across the huge pool to the stairway leading up to the overlook. At the bottom of the steps they paused to catch their breath.

"Do you think Niles went back and closed the box later?" Peter whispered.

"Probably not," Philip replied softly. "I saw him out here working most of the afternoon. He was setting up tables and laying down the stage for the pool party. He didn't look too happy— he wasn't getting much help from anyone else."

After a brief pause, the boys chugged up the stairs, following the flashlight beam and the half-light of the moon. Up on the concrete overlook, they headed straight for the AUTHORIZED PERSONS ONLY sign, squeezed through the iron railings, and located the trail. Even though the night air was cool, both boys were sweating by the time they had slid down the slope and made their way to the spot where they had first seen Niles.

"There it is," said Philip, shining his flashlight beam at the dark square box in the near distance. "I knew it!" he chirped happily. "He left the door open. Come on!"

The boys pushed through the low shrubs to get over to the box, stepping carefully to make sure they didn't accidentally slip off the edge of the wall. Once at the box, Philip swept the flashlight beam across the switches, finally stopping at a large lever that had the simple word *outlet* inscribed on a plate below it.

"Let me do it!" Peter insisted, reaching for the lever and yanking it before Philip had a chance to argue.

There was a click as electric current flowed through the circuit, then a low hum. Peter lifted his hand off the lever and checked his watch. "Three-eighteen. The pool should be half empty by the time anyone wakes up."

"It's going to be awful hard to have a half-pool party!" Philip said, bursting into an evil laugh. "Come on, let's get out of here."

Peter nodded, then giggled as he exchanged high-fives with his terrible twin before they scurried back though the bushes and up the hillside. Scampering across the courtyard, still full of excitement over what they agreed was the greatest stunt they had ever pulled, the boys raced down the stone steps and paused at the bottom, once again to catch their breath.

"It doesn't look like the water is going down," Peter said, looking at the pool in the moonlight.

"I know," Philip agreed, as he shined his light at the water and saw it rising slowly over the lip of the pool. "In fact, I think the water's coming *in*."

Suddenly Philip's eyes widened and he grabbed his brother by the arm. "Hey! When you threw the switch, did you hear the water splash out from the pipe the way it did before?"

"N-no," Peter stammered, fear creeping into his voice.

Then both boys looked down at their feet at the same time as water from the overflowing pool began rising around their sandaled feet

"We'd better get across the bridges back to the hotel," Philip said in a worried voice. "I don't know how deep the water is going to get. It could flood—" He stopped and looked down as the water rose to his knees. "Oh, man! It's really coming in!"

"But how can water that was *below* the pipe we saw today come *into* the pool?" Peter asked. Then suddenly he stiffened as he realized the answer to his question. "Philip, we better get back to the room. The water's gonna get deep—*fast*!"

"How do you know?" Philip asked.

"Because the tide was low when we saw the pipe before," Peter explained. "It's high tide now! The water from the bay has already risen above the top of the pipe!" On the verge of tears, Peter started to run toward the main building, but the waist-high water was holding him back.

"*Swim!!*" Philip yelled, as both boys realized at the same time that that was their only option if they hoped to get back to safety.

In minutes, the water was lapping against their armpits as the rising tide from the bay flowed into the huge crater. Swimming with all their might, splashing, puffing, and gulping salty water, the two brothers headed across the now totally submerged star-shaped pool toward the hotel.

Philip, who was a better swimmer than his brother and already twenty yards ahead of Peter, had just crossed over the central part of the pool when he saw several large, dark shapes rise up from the bottom. They were coming toward him . . . and they were shaped like large footballs!

In a terrible flash, Philip understood that the incredible power of millions of gallons of water pushing in from the bay had pulled the sharks through the gigantic pipe, forcing them through the filtering area and emptying them into the pool! It was his last complete thought before they struck.

"Peter!" he screamed, flailing his arms in the water to get his brother's attention.

But instead of attracting Peter, Philip's splashing drew a huge bull shark right to him. It hit at his waist, its jagged teeth slicing through his soft belly as though cutting custard. In shock, Philip looked at the pool of blood around him. Then the humpbacked killing machine struck again. With no time to scream, Philip was dragged under the rising water, helplessly punching the beast with his balled-up fist.

Watching in horror as his twin disappeared in a swirl of blood, Peter screamed, "*Philip!!!*" then cried hysterically as he

began to swim for his life toward the hotel. He felt the water lifting him, and for a moment he thought he might actually reach safety . . . until a black-tipped fin surfaced a few feet away.

The bull shark struck him in midstroke. Like his brother, Peter had no time to scream. Instantly, he felt a crushing pressure from his armpit to his belly button as the air rushed from his punctured lungs like a leaking balloon. Then he was yanked beneath the water, punching helplessly at the 600-pound creature and gushing blood that mixed with that of his identical brother.

Minutes later, the water rose to its high point, nearly eight feet above the level of the pool. Umbrellas floated like jellyfish on the surface of the water. Bridges and walkways, totally submerged, looked like a network of underwater highways. And deck chairs and tables, too heavy to reach the surface, floated in limbo a foot or two above the pool decking. The pool had become a huge lagoon, still as glass now—except for the ripples trailing behind the fins of the nervous, caged sharks as they searched for a way back to the bay.

The shriek of an alarm clock awakened Mr. and Mrs. Huckabee from a sound sleep at 6:30 in the morning. They'd planned to slip out for a sunrise swim before the boys woke up—the twins had always been late sleepers.

Mrs. Huckabee stretched, then got out of bed and walked to the bedroom's balcony overlooking the pool. "Honey?" she said in a confused voice. "Could you come here for a minute?"

Mr. Huckabee sat up and yawned. "Something wrong,

dear?" he asked, detecting an odd tone in her voice.

"The pool. It's . . . not there," she said haltingly.

"You mean there's no water in it?" Mr. Huckabee asked, suddenly feeling uncomfortable.

"No, just the opposite. There's lots of water. In fact, the pool area—the whole star—it's *under*water."

Mr. Huckabee stepped out onto the balcony and looked down. Niles, Laura, and other staff members were gathered on the hillside above what had once been the pool. Beside them were what looked like football-shaped bodies of several large fish. "What the—? How could that happen?" Mr. Huckabee stopped and looked at his wife. *"The boys!"* they cried in unison.

Running across the suite to the boys' bedroom, the Huckabees screamed when they found the room empty. Not knowing whether to be angry or afraid, they quickly dressed and raced out into the hall. A crowd of guests waiting for the elevator was buzzing about what had happened.

Mr. and Mrs. Huckabee looked at each other in horror. They were both thinking the same thing—their boys *had* to be involved.

When the elevator came they crowded in with everybody else and took it down to the main lobby, which was filled with hysterical guests. They headed for the pool area but stopped short when they saw water lapping against the short set of steps that led down to it.

"If those kids pulled some crazy stunt . . ." Mr. Huckabee said, his face reddening. "I'll—well, I don't know what I'll do!"

But Mrs. Huckabee ignored him. She was looking at Niles floating across the pool area in an aluminum boat, the barrel of a large hunting rifle poking up out of the stern. She watched as the man rowed toward something and reached over the side. Then he pulled whatever it was out from among the floating umbrellas that drifted in the area.

Now Mrs. Huckabee was running out of the doorway, skirting the edge of the pinkish-blue water. Somewhere deep inside she knew something was terribly wrong. She reached the hillside where the staff had gathered just as Niles arrived.

"What are those?" Laura was asking, as she pointed at what Niles had in the bottom of the boat.

"I . . . uh . . . I think you'd better take Mrs. Huckabee inside, Laura," Niles said.

"NO! NO!" Mrs. Huckabee shrieked, pushing through the gathering crowd and looking down into the bottom of the boat. There, lying in a pool of bloody water, were two human arms— a right and left—each with digital watches blinking at the same time, in identical rhythm.

The Last Wave

Ryan Mitchell squats on the smooth pebbles of Hideaway Beach and watches his older brother, Todd, walk into the waist-high surf of Half Moon Bay. Todd wades past the small waves and slaps his surfboard onto the murky, gray-green water. Then he slides belly-first onto the board and paddles through the foamy swells toward the bigger waves a hundred yards out.

As he watches Todd thrust his wet-suited arms shoulder-deep into the salty water, effortlessly gliding the fluorescent green board through the chilly bay, Ryan admires the strength and power in his brother's stroke. *Will my arms and back ever be that strong?* Ryan wonders. He can't even imagine ever being as lean and athletic as Todd—at eighteen, already the best surfer Half Moon Bay has ever known.

The bright sunlight bouncing off the waves forces Ryan to squint as he follows his brother's path into deeper water. He shades his eyes and sees that Todd has reached the next line of waves at the inlet where large, eight-foot crests break into smaller pieces and run to the beach. Todd is now sitting upright on his board, rising and falling in the swelling water like a fishing bobber, waiting for the perfect wave to carry him back to the shallows.

Listening to sea lions honk on the dark, jagged ledges and jutting rocks that ring the tiny strip of beach, Ryan imagines himself out there, impressing all the girls. *Well, maybe when I'm bulked up a little,* he thinks. *Maybe when I'm a little more like Todd.*

Half Moon Bay, Ryan knows, is a tough spot to surf. The water is practically frigid, and the tide running out of the narrow, crescent-shaped bay could carry an inexperienced surfer halfway to Santa Cruz. Also, sharks come into the bay, swimming very close to shore, when their favorite food—sea lions-—come each spring to mate and have pups. Ryan has heard dozens of stories of bitten boards and sharks mistaking surfers for seals. In fact, the stories are told like legends among the surfing crowd, but they always make Ryan shudder.

As one of the horrible stories pops into his mind, Ryan's thoughts are suddenly broken by the flash of Todd's Day-Glo green board shooting to the water's surface. Grabbing his high-powered binoculars, Ryan leaps up to get a better look at his brother, who has caught a huge wave.

His body crouched, Todd centers his weight as the swelling water lifts and propels him shoreward. Ryan watches in awe as the ocean rises behind Todd and carries him in its huge, watery palm.

But all of a sudden, Todd banks right and the board noses up and over the white froth. Like a cowboy jumping into the saddle, Ryan's show-off brother has straddled his board and now raises his arm skyward, twirling an imaginary lariat. "Darn you, Todd," Ryan mutters under his breath, as he realizes his brother is just goofing around. "What a ham."

"Yeeee-haw! Yeeeeeee-haw!" Todd's deep voice cuts through the crashing surf. He shakes his long blond hair out of his eyes and waves at Ryan, who waves back.

In the bright sunlight, Ryan can hardly see the stump where Todd's arm ends just above the wrist. The wet suit covers his other scars, so anyone else on the beach would see only a free-spirited surfer. But Ryan remembers the ribbons of flesh, the torn tissue, and splintered bone that was once his brother's body. Ryan remembers the terrible hulking shape rising from the murky waters, the gushing fountains of blood, and the throat-ripping screams of pain that rose from his brother's throat. It's amazing Todd's alive, let alone surfing again . . . out there.

It had happened not even a full two years ago, in spring, when sea lion rookeries were filled with crying pups, and sea cows spent their days trying to keep their young fed. The rocks around Half Moon Bay practically glistened from the fur of thousands of the sleek, barking seal lions, and macho sea bulls made all kinds of noise fighting over their mates.

Todd had outfitted his van for a camping and surfing weekend. A rack for boards had been bolted on the roof, and the floor had been covered with foam padding, just right for sacking out on. He'd even bought a propane lantern and stove, and the huge cooler was stocked with every kind of soda, not to mention enormous submarine sandwiches.

Todd and his buddies were going to the perfect surfer's escape in Hideaway Beach. With its rocky shore and bone-chilling water, Hideaway kept the swimsuit crowd away. Only a few kids at school even knew about it, and it had become like a private surfer's club.

Ryan could hardly believe it when Todd had asked him to come along—and his parents had said okay. The brothers had always been pretty tight, even though Todd was four years older. But Ryan never dreamed he'd be hanging out and surfing with the coolest guys in school.

Actually, Ryan wasn't much of a surfer. He liked the ocean, and he knew a lot more than most kids about marine life, but he'd never been able to catch a wave and ride a curl like Todd and the older guys. Ryan just wasn't very athletic, nor was he very strong. His knees wobbled every time he tried to move on the board to steer it, and he fell more often than not. The truth was, Ryan was more interested in what was happening *under* the waves than on top of them, and he knew that Todd had only invited him to tag along to psych him up about surfing. "You've just got to center your mind and body," Todd would always say. "You've got to be lifted by the power of the ocean."

The only problem was that the ocean didn't cooperate that day. The weather had been perfect, all right—sunny and clear, with a breeze blowing down from the Santa Cruz mountains—but the waves were tiny, choppy, and totally useless to a surfer. Todd and his buddies waited, their wet suits zipped, their surfboards bobbing like corks in the gentle heaves, but the breeze kept the surf down, and by Sunday morning most of the campers had packed up their boards and headed home.

But not Todd. He had been determined to surf and determined to show his little brother how to ride the waves. "I'm not leaving until I get the waves I came here for," he'd told Ryan. "We're going to surf together if it's the last thing I do."

Ryan had wanted to go home—not because he'd given up on surfing, but because he was afraid. On an early morning walk along the beach, he'd seen a large brown lump at the foot of the rocky cliffs. As he'd gotten closer, he'd seen a buzzing cloud of green flies rising over what he'd soon come to realize was the smelly remains of an enormous sea lion—a bull, probably ten feet long. Actually, it was hard to tell how big the animal had been, because only the top half of the carcass—from just below the first flipper up to the snout—had washed up on the beach. Below the fins, a gooey, purplish mass of blubber and guts wriggling with maggots spilled onto the dark sand, and Ryan felt his stomach heave. He knew right away what had happened. Something had bitten the sea lion completely in half.

Todd had just shrugged when Ryan told him about the mangled carcass. "Probably got run over by a boat," he'd said. "Come on. Let's paddle out past the point. The breeze is really coming off the water today."

Ryan knew that a boat couldn't cut a sea lion in half—chew it up, maybe; take chunks from its flesh, sure; but it couldn't slice through hundreds of pounds of fat and sever a spinal cord. Only one thing could do that, and it wasn't an engine—it had to be an eating machine . . . like a great white shark.

Still, somehow Todd had convinced him to go, and with his teeth chattering, Ryan paddled out toward the deeper water, just barely keeping up with Todd's powerful strokes. It was a warm day, but the fear that had passed through Ryan's bones at the sight of the mangled seal had left a tremor in his body that he could not control.

Finally, Todd had stopped paddling and straddled his board almost a hundred yards from the beach. Ryan pulled up next to him and remained belly-first on the board as he positioned it toward shore. *Please let a good wave come quickly,* he'd thought, *so Todd can get this out of his system and we can go home.* But the murky, greenish-gray water simply rose and fell like a giant's soft breathing, gently lifting and lowering their boards.

Thwack! Thwack!

Ryan winced, remembering how Todd had slammed the water in frustration. "I'll just have to make my own waves!" his feisty brother had yelled.

Ryan had looked over at Todd nervously. "I don't think it's such a good idea to do that. You never know what's down there. Sometimes sharks—"

"Get off this shark thing, Ryan!" Todd had snapped, looking at Ryan like he was a total wimp. "More people get hit by lightning every year than get bitten by sharks."

That's because people stay inside during thunderstorms— they don't go looking for lightning, Ryan had thought. In fact, he would remember thinking that for the rest of his life.

Thwack! Thwack!

Todd had slapped the water again, as if taunting the ocean to cooperate. "I'm not quitting," he'd told Ryan. "If you want to paddle in, go ahead. I'm waiting for the waves."

And so Todd had turned his board toward deeper waters. "I'll see you later, chicken," he'd said, raising his arm to wave.

Ryan had seen the shark hit before Todd had even lowered his arm. The water seemed to boil around his brother's board as the huge gray shape rose from the bottom and hit like a runaway train—a train with jaws like two monstrous chain saws.

Once again Ryan winced, remembering how Todd's feet had suddenly pointed to the sky as the creature flipped him and began to drag him under. And, oh, how Todd had fought! He'd battled to the surface several times, and had even looked at Ryan, his mouth forming a distorted oval as he'd screamed in shock and terror. Then, without warning, Todd had vanished, yanked below to the ocean depths with his arms flailing like a rag doll, the churning waters turning a hideous red.

And what had *he* done? Ryan now thought with a sick feeling rising in his stomach. He'd frozen, but not before a cool wave of vomit had risen from his stomach. Sure, he'd finally fought off every urge in his body to flee; and yes, he'd finally forced himself to paddle toward the bloody, foaming water twenty yards away. But then he'd frozen again when he'd seen Todd rise from the water, the upper half of his body zooming along the surface, while the lower half remained tight in the shark's hideous grip.

It was all still so clear in Ryan's memory. In that frozen moment, he'd seen the white stripes of his brother's splintered ribs through his shredded wet suit. And he'd seen how Todd had reached out to him, grunting in pain, unable even to scream because the air had been driven from his lungs. And how could

Ryan ever forget how he'd given a quick thrust with his board so he could reach out for Todd's hand . . . which came off above the wrist, leaving only shattered bone and gory ribbons of tissue at the end of the arm.

"No!" Ryan had screamed, his eyes wide in horror as he saw the huge gray shape rising from the dark background to claim another piece of Todd. Then, with a violent scream that rose from the core of his body, Ryan had kicked out at the shark's snout, hoping to distract it away from his brother.

But suddenly, it was *he* who had felt a searing pain. For when he had kicked at the shark, his leg had driven into the huge cavern that was the shark's mouth. Ryan remembered looking straight down at the beast's triangular teeth set in rows, like thousands of three-inch bayonets.

"No! No! No!" he'd screamed over and over, each time hammering the shark's mouth with every ounce of strength he had. Pain had rushed through him as the monster's rough scales tore into his wet flesh, but the last blow had definitely loosened its hold on his leg, and Ryan had pulled free.

"Todd!" he'd yelled, as the terrible shark sank beneath the waves again.

And then Ryan had spotted him. Only about five feet away, there was Todd, thrashing in the darkening water, trying somehow to swim from the agony. Making a desperate lunge for his brother, Ryan had managed to get his fingers on a torn flap of Todd's wet suit. Then, just before Todd sank beneath the water, Ryan had hauled his mangled body out of the surf and had placed his arm across Todd's groaning chest in a lifeguard's carry. Paddling with his free arm, praying out loud that the shark had left to look for other prey, Ryan had headed to shore.

After what had seemed like a lifetime, Ryan's feet had finally touched sand, and he'd dragged his brother's torn body onto the beach. Exhausted, still in shock himself, he'd crawled over to the towels they had left only a half-hour earlier, wrapped one around the gushing wound on his own leg, and then scrambled back to Todd with the other.

Covered with so much blood that it was impossible to see his wounds, Todd had lain nearly lifeless on the beach. Ryan had gently put the towel over his brother and knelt by his side. Placing his left hand on Todd's ribs to hold them in place, he'd begun mouth-to-mouth resuscitation when, like a godsend, a helicopter had appeared in the distance.

Mrs. Mitchell waits in the driveway as Ryan pulls the van in. "Ryan! Where have you been?" she asks impatiently. "Dad and I have been worried sick!"

Ryan smiles. "I was at Hideaway, Mom."

"You *drove* all the way to Hideaway?" Mrs. Mitchell sputters. "You can't drive that far yet, honey. You *know* that."

Ryan slides awkwardly out of the driver's seat. His eyes shine happily. "I saw Todd, Mom. I saw him there."

Mrs. Mitchell looks at the ground and shakes her head. She looks back up at her son, with tears streaming down her face. "Ryan, honey, we've been going to Dr. Bransfield to talk about this for two years now."

"But Mom, Todd was—"

"No, Ryan. Todd *wasn't*. Todd is dead."

"But I saved him, Mom!" Ryan's voice rises in panic. "I pulled him to the beach. I covered him with—"

"No, Ryan. We never found Todd. You know that. We talk about this each week with the doctor." Mrs. Mitchell sighs. "When the fishermen found you, you had almost bled to death yourself. Remember, honey?"

Ryan begins to cry. "Yes . . . yes, I remember."

"And what did you have, Ryan?" Mrs. Mitchell asks gently.

"Todd's hand," he whispers. "I—I had Todd's hand in my hand."

Ryan looks at the ground. His shoulders heave and tears run off his nose, splashing on the plastic limb just below his knee to his shoe.

"Come on, honey." Mrs. Mitchell puts her arm around Ryan's waist. "Let's go inside. Don't cry. Once you learn how to use that leg a little better, you can drive anyplace you want—even to Hideaway."